JOSEPH ROTH

The Silent Prophet

Translated by David Le Vay

THE OVERLOOK PRESS
Woodstock, New York

Translated from the German
Der Stumme Prophet

First published in the United States in 1980 by
The Overlook Press
Lewis Hollow Road
Woodstock, New York 12498
Copyright © 1966 by
Verlag Kiepenheuer & Witsch-Cologne-Berlin and
Verlag Allert de Lange-Amsterdam
English translation © Peter Owen Ltd 1979

Library of Congress Cataloging in Publication Data

Roth, Joseph, 1894-1939.
The silent prophet.

Translation of Der stumme Prophet.
I. Title.
PZ3.R7428Si   1980   [PT2635.084]   833'.912   79-67676
ISBN 0-87951-110-9

Printed in U.S.A.

Prologue

On New Year's Eve 1926-1927 I was sitting with some friends and acquaintances in Moscow in room Number Nine of the Bolshaia Moskovskaia Hotel. For some of those present this private mode of celebrating the New Year was the only one possible. Their views would clearly have permitted them a public expression of festive spirit. But certain considerations had to be taken into account, and to be feared. They could mix neither with foreigners nor with the local citizens and although each and every one of them had functioned long and often as an observer to further an idea, he rightly shunned becoming himself the object of observation.

In my room there floated the haze of cigarette smoke familiar to those acquainted with the novels of Russian literature. I opened intermittently the small transom of the window – my guests had restrained me from opening the entire window – and presently the door, which led into the corridor and through which entered the sounds of music, voices, glasses, footsteps, song.

'Do you realize,' said Grodzki, a Ukrainian Pole who had worked for a long time for the Cheka in Tokyo, and for whom I had developed a certain fellow feeling when he approached me with the request to write some reports about me and I had replied at once that I still recalled his activities in Japan. . . . 'Do you realize,' asked Grodzki, 'who used to live here three years ago, in this very room, Number Nine?' A few regarded him questioningly. For a few seconds he made the most of the silence. Like many of those who had been employed in the secret service, he craved not only to know something but to have known

7

about it longer than anyone else. 'Kargan,' he said after a pause. 'Oh, him!' exclaimed B., a journalist whose orthodoxy was well-known. 'Why so scornful?' said Grodzki. 'Because we have probably already harboured several of his kind here, in this room Number Nine,' replied B. with a glance in my direction.

The others joined in. Almost all professed to have known Kargan and almost all expressed a more or less critical view of him. The appellations invented by orthodox theory for revolutionaries with an intellectual past are familiar and I need hardly rehearse the meaning of the wording of each. 'Anarchist,' exclaimed one, 'sentimental rebel,' another, 'intellectual individualist,' a third.

I may possibly have seized the opportunity to defend Kargan rather too eagerly just then. Although I suspected him at that time of being in Paris, and not without reason, I felt quite unaccountably as if he were now my guest and that it was my duty to protect him. Possibly Grodzki's information that Kargan had lived in this room of mine years before provoked me to a long speech in his defence. It was not, in fact, a speech. It was a history. It was an attempt at a biography. Apart from Grodzki, whose vocation compelled him to know everybody, I was the best placed of all those present to know everything about the man attacked. I began my narration, supported by Grodzki, and both of us did not finish that night. I continued the story the next night and the third night; but by the third night the listeners had dwindled to two. They were the only ones not officially obliged or afraid to hear the truth.

In consequence I felt it necessary for my narrative to reach a more extensive audience than my voice could provide. I decided to write down what I had been recounting.

Kargan's life is described below, set out in the same sequence as it was recounted then. The interruptions of the listeners, their gestures, their jokes, their questions, are omitted. Omitted too, even deliberately suppressed, are certain indications that might lead to Kargan's identification and might further the reader's natural impulse to recognize in the individual portrayed a definite, historically existing personality. Kargan's life-story is as little related to actual events as any other. It is not intended to exemplify a political point of view – at most, it demonstrates the old and eternal truth that the individual is always defeated in the end.

Is Friedrich Kargan destined finally to sink into oblivion?

In the light of news of him received by some of his friends, indirectly but reliably, some weeks ago, he seems to have abandoned any intention to seek out the civilized part of the world of his own accord. It is therefore possible that one day he will be engulfed in empty solitude, un-noticed and without trace, like a falling star in a silent obscure night. Then his end would remain unknown, as until now were his early beginnings.

Book One

I

Friedrich was born in Odessa, in the house of his grand-father, Kargan, the rich tea merchant. He was an un-wanted, because illegitimate, child, the son of an Austrian piano-teacher named Zimmer to whom the rich tea merchant had refused his daughter. The piano-teacher vanished from Russia, old Kargan had him sought for in vain after he had learned of his daughter's pregnancy.

Six months later he sent her and the new-born child to his brother, a wealthy merchant in Trieste. In this man's home Friedrich spent his childhood. It passed not altogether unhappily, even though he had fallen into the hands of a benefactor.

Only when his mother died – at an early age and of a disease that was never accurately identified – was Friedrich quartered in a servant's room. On holidays and special occasions he was allowed to eat at the same table as the children of the house. He preferred the company of the domestics, from whom he learned the pleasures of life and a distrust of the lords and masters.

At primary school he proved far more gifted than the children of his benefactor. Therefore the latter did not allow him to continue his education but apprenticed him to a shipping agent's, where Friedrich had the prospect, after several years, of becoming a skilled official with a monthly wage of a hundred and twenty kronen.

At that time a growing number of deserters, emigrants and refugees from the pogroms were crossing the Austrian border from Russia. The shipping agencies therefore began to set up branch establishments in the border states of the

Monarchy to intercept the emigrants and despatch them to Brazil, Canada and the United States.

These branch agencies enjoyed the goodwill of the authorities. It was the government's unconcealed desire to remove these poor, unemployed and not altogether innocuous refugees from Austria as quickly as possible; but also to convey the impression that Russian deserters would be supplied with sailing tickets and recommendations to countries overseas – to such an extent that the desire to quit the army should affect an increasing number of Russian malcontents. The authorities were probably tipped off not to keep too close an eye on the shipping agents.

However, it was not easy to find reliable and skilled staff for the frontier establishments. The older employees did not want to leave their districts, homes and families. In addition, they were unfamiliar with the languages, manners and inhabitants of the border territories. Lastly, they were also scared of a somewhat risky occupation.

In the office where Friedrich worked he was regarded as capable and diligent. He mastered several languages, among them Russian. He was a thoughtful young man. What was not appreciated was that his quiet and always alert courtesy concealed a shrewd and silent arrogance. His taciturn pride was taken for reserve. However, he hated his superiors, his instructors, his benefactor and every kind of authority. He was timid, did not participate in sports with those of his own age, he dealt no blows and received none, evaded every danger, and his fearfulness always exceeded his curiosity. He prepared to revenge himself on the world which, he believed, treated him as a second-class person. It thwarted his ambition that he could not go to high school like his fellows and cousins. He made up his mind to complete his studies one day nevertheless, to enter the high school and become a statesman, politician, diplomat – in any case someone powerful. When it was suggested to him that he should go to one of the border subsidiaries, he immediately assented, in the hope of a lucky change of fortune and an interruption of the normal routine, which he detested. On this first journey he took with him his foresight, his cunning, and his ability to dissemble, qualities bestowed on him by nature.

Before he climbed into the passenger train which left for the east, he cast a yearning and yet reproachful glance at an elegant coffee-coloured international sleeping-car which was due to depart from Trieste for Paris.

'One day I shall be one of the passengers in that coach,' thought Friedrich.

2

Forty-eight hours later he arrived at the little border town where the Parthagener family ran a branch of the shipping agency. Old Parthagener had owned the inn, 'The Ball and Chain', for over forty years. It was the first house on the wide street that ran from the frontier to the town. Here the fugitives and deserters came and encountered the pure and calm serenity of the old man with the silver beard, who seemed to be a manifestation of nature's blind intent ultimately to clothe all men, irrespective of their sins or deserts, with the white colour of dignity. Over his weak and light-sensitive eyes Herr Parthagener wore blue spectacles. They merely deepened further the serenity of his face and were reminiscent of a dark curtain over the window of a bright and luminous house-front. The agitated refugees at once placed their trust in the old man and left him a good part of the possessions they had brought with them.

The three Parthagener sons had an official, even nautical, appearance, thanks to their white sailor-hats and armbands of navy blue. They distributed among the emigrants illustrated prospectuses inviting one to contemplate dark-green meadows, brindled cows, cabins with blue smoke rising, endless fields of tobacco and rice. From the prospectuses wafted an air of lush and peaceful surfeit. The refugees became homesick for South America and the Parthageners sold steamship tickets.

Not all the emigrants possessed the necessary papers. Thus they were turned back on their arrival in foreign parts. They remained confined in mass hutments, endured one disinfection after another, and finally embarked on a long tour of the police cells of several countries. However, for those who could pay, papers were manufactured at the frontier. A man named Kapturak supplied the circumspect and well-to-do with false documents.

Who was Kapturak? A diminutive man with a greenish-grey complexion, spindly limbs, deft movements, a quack doctor and a shady lawyer by calling, renowned as a smuggler and on good terms with the border officials. His smuggling of goods was only a cover for his traffic in human beings. The many terms he served in the various jails of the territory were his voluntary concessions to the law. Every year, in spring, he appeared at the frontier like a bird of passage. He emerged from one of the many jails of the interior. The snow melted. It rained warm and fragrant in the veiled nights. And the frontier slept. One could cross it silently and invisibly.

During the months of February, March and April he worked. In May he sat in the train in broad daylight with his pack of uncustomed wares, pretended to escape from the inspectors and allowed himself to be imprisoned. Sometimes he treated himself to a vacation and travelled to Karlsbad, for the good of his stomach.

He and the Parthagener family worked together. In the morning, an hour after sunrise, he would bring his protégés to 'The Ball and Chain'. They would pay for three days' board and lodging in advance. At this point a young Parthagener would appear with prospectuses.

From time to time, however, someone from the agency had to make a so-called 'spot-check', at night, across the frontier. For it occasionally happened that Kapturak led his fugitives to another town, to other Parthageners, in other inns, handed them over to other branches of the firm. So one had to catch him unawares on Russian territory, in the so-called 'border taverns'.

Friedrich arrived at the Parthageners' on a sunny day in March 1908. There was a steady cheerful drip from the icicles on the gutters. The sky was light blue. Old Parthagener sat in front of his inn door. A dirty dark-grey crust lay over the large piles of snow on either side of the high-road. The winter was beginning to break up.

Friedrich was young enough to note all the processes of nature and relate them to his experiences. He drank in the special light of this day. It was strong like the warm young south-west wind, the darkness of the crooked gateway and the silvered dignity of the old man.

'He might as well bring a "batch" across next week!' said the ancient to his sons, who were standing at the open window in their gleaming white sailor-hats.

'Come along in,' he then said to Friedrich, 'and have something to drink!'

From then on Friedrich remained at 'The Ball and Chain'.

3

A week later he was sent to the border tavern to bring a 'batch' across. The train had arrived at eleven at night, they were not due to cross the frontier until three in the morning. Four deserters slept huddled together on the floor, a double row of bodies, heads on their bundles. Behind the counter sat the deaf and dumb landlord. He opened his eyes wide, for they served him instead of ears and he could hear with them. But now there was nothing to hear. Kapturak had nodded off in a chair. Against the door, haggard and menacing, leaned the swarthy Caucasian, Savelli. He refused to sit down, he was afraid of falling asleep. He mistrusted Kapturak. The authorities would have been prepared to pay a high price for Savelli. Who knew whether Kapturak might not intend to turn him in?

The adventurousness of this nocturnal hour intrigued no one but Friedrich. For those who had been engaged in smuggling for years it was usual and ordinary. It was not until years later and in distant lands that the deserters, who were now overcome by fatigue, would remember the weirdness of this place between death and freedom, and the stillness of the encircling night in the midst of which this tavern was the only lighted place, the bright focus of an immense darkness. Only Friedrich listened to the regular slow ticking of a clock which counted out its seconds as if time consisted of the costly drops of a rare and noble metal. Only he observed the large sluggish flies on the wide petroleum lamp whose wick was turned down to a narrow strip and whose broad shade of brown cardboard darkened the upper half of the room. And only he noted the distant whistle of a locomotive which resounded in the night like a frightened man's call for help.

Towards two in the morning another whistle sounded, cut short, suppressed, fearful. Kapturak heard it. He jumped up and woke the sleepers. Each put his bundle on his back. They went outside. The night was dim and humid, the ground moist. The steps of each were audible. They went through a wood. Kapturak stood still. 'Lie down!' he whispered, and all quietly lay down. A twig snapped.

After a while Kapturak jumped up and began to run. 'Follow me!' he shouted. Behind him they all jumped over a ditch. They continued running to the edge of the wood. Behind them a shot rang out and died away in a long echo.

They were over the border. The men walked slowly, silently, heavily. Each one's breathing could be heard. Friedrich could not see them but he remembered their faces clearly, simple snub-nosed peasant faces, eyes under puny foreheads, massive trunks and heavy limbs.

He loved them, for he was sensitive to their distress. He thought of the innumerable frontiers of the gigantic empire. This very night hundreds of thousands were leaving, moving from misfortune to misfortune. The boundless silent

19

night was peopled with human fugitives, flattened wretched faces, massive trunks, heavy limbs.

It began to lighten in the east. As if by command they all suddenly stood still and turned back in the direction from which they had come, as if the night they were abandoning had become their homeland and the dawn only a frontier. They stood still and bade farewell to their homeland, to a farm, an animal, a mother, this one to a hundred acres and another to a single strip of ground, to the striking of a particular clock, the crow of a cock, the creaking of a familiar door. They stood there as if conducting some rite. Suddenly Savelli began to sing a soldier's song in a strong clear voice. All joined in and sang with him. They still had a good hour to go to reach Parthagener's inn.

4

'That is probably his hymn of praise,' said Kapturak rather loudly to Friedrich. Though everyone was singing Savelli heard the remark and retorted: 'Of the two of us, Kapturak, you are the one who should be singing a hymn of praise! You can thank God that you didn't hand me over. I would have killed you.'

'I know,' said Kapturak, 'and I should not have been the first or the last. Is it true that you did away with Kalashvili?'

'I was around,' replied Savelli. It sounded mysterious.

However, Savelli did not give the impression that he had anything to conceal in the affair.

'I saw him die,' he went on. 'I never for a moment thought that he also had a private life, outside his police duties. Anyway, he could not have continued to live in peace. I don't believe in the peace of a traitor.'

'You must have hated him,' Friedrich ventured to ask.

'No!' replied Savelli. 'I did not feel hate. I believe one can only hate if one has suffered personally at the hands of another. But I'm not capable of that. I am a tool. People use my head, my hands, my constitution. My life is not my own. I no longer belong to myself. I would have to transgress the rights befitting a tool if I wanted to hate him. Or love him, even!'

'But you *do* love?'

'What?'

'I mean,' answered Friedrich slowly, for he was shy of using a large word, 'the Idea, the Revolution.'

'I have worked eight years for it,' said Savelli quietly, 'and cannot say sincerely whether I love it. Is it possible to love something that is so much bigger than I am? I don't understand how believers can love God! I think of love as a force which can grasp and possess its object. No! I don't believe that I love the Revolution – not in that sense.'

'One can love God,' uttered Kapturak decisively.

'Maybe a believer sees him,' opined Savelli. 'Maybe I ought to see the Revolution. . . .'

'If you run away,' said Kapturak, 'who will make the Revolution?'

'Who needs make it?' cried Savelli. 'It's coming. Your children will see it.'

'God help my children !' said Kapturak.

Friedrich knew who Savelli was. He figured under the name of Tomyshkin in the newspaper reports. He had carried out the notorious bank-raids and illegal movement of money in the Caucasus and in south-west Russia. The police had sought hirr ior years in va. .,

'He could have stayed on longer,' remarked Kapturak. 'He wasn't worried about the police. But they need him abroad.'

Savelli remained at the inn for a few days. 'Are you related to the Parthageners?' he once asked Friedrich. And when Friedrich denied this, 'Then what are you doing in the company of these bandits?'

'I must save money in order to learn,' said Friedrich. 'Soon I shall return to Vienna.'

'Then come and see me sometime!' said Savelli. And he gave him his addresses in Vienna, Zürich and London.

Friedrich felt the same kind of embarrassed gratitude for this notorious man that a patient feels for his doctor when he announces the protracted course of a disease with kindness and consideration. Savelli was strange, hard, sinister. Friedrich detested the sacrifice, the anonymity of the sacrifice, the voluntary association the Caucasian cultivated with death.

Life stretched before Friedrich's youth, immense in its extent, incalculably rich in years and adventure. When he set the word 'World' before him, he saw pleasures, women, fame and riches.

He accompanied Savelli to the station. In a single short moment, when Savelli was already standing on the footboard, Friedrich had the feeling that the stranger had assumed control of his youth, his life, his future. He wanted to hand back the addresses and say : 'I shall never look you up.' But now Savelli was holding out his hand. He took it. Savelli smiled. He closed the carriage door. Friedrich watched for a while. Savelli did not return to the window.

5

Friedrich learned how to lie, to forge papers, to exploit the impotence, the stupidity, and even sometimes the brutality of the officials. Others of his age were still dreading a black mark or a bad reference at school. He was already aware that there were no incorruptible persons in the world, that everything could be accomplished with the aid of money and nearly everything with the aid of intelligence. He began to save. In his spare time he prepared for matriculation. To this end he had become acquainted with a law student who had had to leave the university for some undisclosed reason. This student was currently living there as clerk to a solicitor and announced his intention of awaiting a more favourable era. He called himself a 'free revolutionary' and still adhered to the ideals of the French Revolution. He sighed for the one that had failed in 1848. He spoke of the great days in Paris, of the guillotine, of Metternich, of the minister Latour as of recent and immediate matters. He wanted one day to become a politician, an Opposition deputy. And he already possessed the robust, unruffled, solid aggressiveness of a parliamentarian that might well discountenance a suave minister of the old régime. In the meantime he confined his political activities to participation in the meetings which were held twice a week at Chaikin's, the cobbler's.

Chaikin was one of those Russian émigrés whose poverty had prevented him from leaving this border town. Although he earned barely enough for a cup of tea, a piece of bread, a radish, he supported the revolutionaries who came over the border. Every month he expected the outbreak of the world revolution. He prided himself on performing important duties on its behalf and eventually became the head of an impotent conspiracy. Round him gathered the rebellious and dissatisfied. For even in this town, on the periphery of the capitalist world, in which the statute books had only a diminished and debased effect, the unwritten laws of the establishment and of bourgeois morality were nevertheless observed in their full validity. Amidst the striking and unEuropean local colour, in the bizarre tumult of adventurers, doubtful nationalities and the babel of tongues, the putrescent gleam of a patriarchal entrepreneurial benevolence still lingered, the wages of the small artisans and workmen were kept low, the poor were maintained in their submissiveness, which was exposed in the streets beside the infirmities of the beggars. Here, too, those who had settled showed their hatred towards the migrants; all the newly-arrived poor – and some arrived every week – were greeted with the same hostility that the others had themselves received. And even the beggars, who lived on charity, were as afraid of competitors as the shopkeepers. From the officers of the garrison there emanated a metallic glitter to which the daughters of the lower middle class succumbed. At election times soldiers and police moved into the town and spread fear, and the townsfolk were just as cowed as their brethren in the larger European cities.

The rebels met at Chaikin's. In compliance with theory, he called the few municipal watchmen 'capitalist lackeys', a merchant who did not pay his apprentices 'an exploiter and entrepreneur', the town councillors 'beneficiaries of society', the apprentices 'beasts of burden', and 120 brushmakers the 'proletarian masses'. He organized discussions. He expounded the small and the major programmes. He arranged demonstrations on various occasions. Nothing would have made him happier than to be arrested. But no one regarded him as dangerous.

Friedrich attended Chaikin's meetings regularly. He went out of curiosity. He stayed out of ambition. In the discussion he learned how to make his point at any price. He developed his marked talent for false formulations. He enjoyed the hush which settled when he rose to speak, in which he imagined he could hear his voice even before it rang out. For days on end he prepared himself to counter every possible objection. He learned to feign a quickwittedness that he did not really possess. He reproduced strange sentences from pamphlets as if they were his own. He enjoyed triumphs. And yet he sincerely loved the poor folk who listened to him, and the red world conflagration he intended to kindle.

The World! What a word! He heard it with youthful ears. It radiated a great beauty and concealed great injustice. Twice a week he deemed it necessary to destroy it and on the other days he readied himself to conquer it.

To this end he studied so zealously that one day his student friend was able to say :

'I think you could sit the examination in two months' time. See if you can make it this autumn.'

Friedrich counted the money he had saved. It was enough for six months. He consulted Kapturak about documents. There was some satisfaction to be obtained in appearing before the authorities of the capitalist world with false papers. He had no father and no country. His birth had not been registered anywhere. He took this as a sign and went to Kapturak.

'In what names?'

'Friedrich Zimmer.'

'Why Zimmer?'

'That was my father's name.'

'Russian or Austrian?'

'Austrian.'

'Quite right,' said Kapturak. 'A young man should not stay in our town. Go out into the world and study law. That's useful. You may yet be a district commissioner.'

It was on a July day that Freidrich took his departure. The sun beat down on the low roofs of the cottages between which the path led to the station and drove the smoke from the chimneys in front of the low doors. In the middle of the street, which was bordered on both sides by wooden sidewalks, there was a bustle of women and children, peaceful poultry and aggressive dogs. All was pervaded by a fragrant summery influence, and over the smoke from the chimneys prevailed a distant smell of hay and of the trunks of the spruce forest behind the station.

Friedrich was determined to resist any kind of traditional emotion. The fear of melancholy conferred on him the false steadfastness of which young men are unnecessarily proud, and which they take for manliness. He exaggerated the significance of this moment. He had read

26

too much. All of a sudden he re-experienced a hundred scenes of parting. But as the train began to move he forgot the town he was leaving and thought only of that world into which he was travelling.

6

At noon on a fine day in August, a certificate in his pocket, he emerged from the great brown doorway of a Viennese high school. He made his way homeward through the still heat. The streets were empty. They contained only shadows, sun and stones.

He encountered a carriage. The noiseless rubber tyres glided over the paving as if over a polished table. Only a cheerful feudal clatter of horses' hooves could be heard. In the carriage, under a light sunshade currently the fashion, sat a young woman. As she passed by she had time enough to study Friedrich with the protracted and insulting indifference with which one contemplates a tree, a horse or a lamp-post. He passed before her eyes as before a mirror.

'She has no idea,' he thought, 'who I am. My suit is wretched and no wonder; the youngest Parthagener sold it to me cheap. It has a shabby false brightness. The pockets are too deep, the trousers too wide. It's like deceptive sunshine in February. I'm wearing a hat of coarse straw, it presses like heavy wire netting and is spuriously summery. Beautiful women look past me indifferently.'

27

She was a beautiful woman. A narrow nose with delicate nostrils, brown cheeks, a narrow rather over-straight
mouth. Her neck, slender and probably brown, disappeared in the collar of her high-necked dress. A foot
in a dove-grey shoe sat like a bird on the facing seat
cushioned in red velvet. The sunlight flowed over her
body, over the cream-coloured dress and filtered through
the parasol which stretched like a tiny sky over its own
small world. The coachman in his ash-grey livery held
the reins tightly. His forearms hung parallel over his
knees. The almost golden glint of the black horses had a
festive jollity. Their docked tails betrayed a flirtatious
strength. They rose and fell governed by the secret rules
of a rhythm not to be fathomed by pedestrians.

This encounter with a beautiful woman was like the
first encounter with an enemy. Friedrich assessed his
position. He weighed up his forces. He summed them up
and pondered whether he dared to go into battle. He had
just taken a barricade. He had, through a laughable
examination, become fit for society. He could become
anything : a defender of mankind, but also its oppressor;
a general and a minister; a cardinal, a politician, a
people's tribune. Nothing – apart from his clothes –
hindered him from advancing far beyond the position the
young woman might occupy; from becoming idolized by
her and her kind; and from rejecting her. Naturally,
rejecting her.

What a long way for one who was poor and alone!
For one without even a name or papers! Everyone else
was rooted in a home. Everyone else was fixed as fast as
bricks in a wall. They had the precious certainty that
their own downfall would also mean the end of the
others. The streets were quiet and filled with peaceful

sunshine. Closed windows. Lowered blinds. Happiness and love dwelled unalloyed behind the green and yellow curtains. Sons honoured their fathers, mothers understood their children, women embraced their husbands, brothers hugged each other.

He could not divorce himself from this quiet, prosperous, fortunate district in which he happened to be. He made detours as if, by some miracle, he might suddenly find himself in front of his house without having to traverse the noisy dirty streets which led to his lodging. The chimney-stacks of the factories emerged straight behind the roofs. The people had slept in tenements, could not keep their balance and seemed as if drunk. The haste of poverty is frightened and soundless and yet begets an indistinct uproar.

He lodged with a tailor, in a gloomy little room. The window had tarnished panes and opened on the hall. It prevented light from entering and the neighbours from looking in. Sewing machines clattered in the landlord's bedroom. The ironing-board lay across the bed, the dressmaker's dummy was propped against the door, customers were measured in the kitchen and the wife, stuck by the stove with flushed face, scolded the four children at their play.

'If I go to the restaurant first,' reflected Friedrich, 'the family will have eaten by the time I get back. There'll be only the washing-up left to do.'

He entered a small restaurant. A man sat down at his table. His ears were strikingly large and withered as if made of yellow paper, his head batlike.

'I think you must be my neighbour,' said the man. 'Don't you live across the road at Number 36?'

'Yes.'

'I've seen you around for some weeks. Do you always eat here?'

'Sometimes.'

'I suppose you're a student.'

'Not yet! I have to get enrolled first.'

'What kind, may I ask?'

'Don't know yet!'

'I'm an address-writer,' said the man. 'My name is Grünhut. I was a student once too. But I had bad luck.' It was as if he really meant: 'You won't escape that fate either.'

'Do you manage all right?' asked Friedrich.

'As an address-writer! Three heller an envelope. A hundred a day, sometimes a hundred and twenty. I can get work for you too. Willingly! I'd be glad to do so. Is your handwriting good? Come tomorrow!'

They went to a linen warehouse. The book-keeper handed them a list and a hundred and fifty green envelopes.

'Where are you eating tonight?' asked Grünhut. 'Come with me.'

They ate in a cellar. They were given soup made of sausage scraps. A long table. Hurrying rattling spoons. Metal tableware. Noises of lips smacking, spoons scraping, throats gurgling. 'Good soup!' said Grünhut. 'I'll show you about the coffee, we have that across the road, at Grüner's. Soon you won't have to bother any more, you'll be eating in the college refectory. I used to feed there once.'

'I could find myself in the same situation,' said Friedrich.

'What, really? What situation? My situation, of course! Do you really think so? Yes, it's a good thing that I've shown you all these places. I had to discover them myself.'

'Thank you.'

'Oh, not at all! Not at all! When I came out of prison, I was all alone. Wife divorced! Brother a stranger. Didn't know me any more. Apart from Frau Tarka, I didn't know a soul. Her brother was in clink with me. So he recommended me. Connections are what count in our circles too. Do you know Frau Tarka? She's the midwife, just over your tailor's. My room's above yours. I checked. You wouldn't believe how many come to Frau Tarka. Yesterday, for example, Dr D.'s daughter. Six months ago it was the wife of a proper Excellency. And the young men! Sons of public prosecutors and generals! Bring their careless little girls. And all I did was to undo the blouse of the pupil I was teaching geography and history in the sixth form, at the high school in the Floriangasse, a private school. Good children from good homes. A working man's daughter wouldn't have said anything. But the well-off! I know a lawyer who raped his ward. A lieutenant who sleeps with his batman. I could write them each a little anonymous letter if I were a scoundrel. But I'm not, in spite of everything. Where do you stand politically? Left, of course! What? I've no opinions. But I think a revolution would do us good. A small short revolution. Three days, for instance.'

A peculiar relationship developed between Friedrich and myself at that time. I might call it intimacy without friendship or comradeship without affection. And even the fellow-feeling which later linked us was not present at the outset. It arose from the attention we began to pay each other one day and from the mutual mistrust we detected in each other. Finally we began to respect each other. Trust grew slowly, was fostered by the glances we exchanged, almost without realizing it, in the company of others and less by the words that passed than by the silences in which we often sat and strolled together. Had our lives not taken such differing courses, Friedrich would probably have become my friend, as did Franz Tunda.

It was a long time before Friedrich decided to look up Savelli, who was still living in Vienna at that time. He was afraid. He felt that, for the time being, he still had the choice between what he termed 'revolutionary asceticism' and the 'world', the vague romantic notion of pleasures, struggles, triumphs. Already he hated the governance of this world, but he still believed in it.

The finely soaring ramp of the University did not yet seem to him – as it did to me – the fortress wall of the national students' association, from which every few weeks Jews or Czechs were flung down, but as a kind of ascent to 'Knowledge and Power'. He had the respect of the self-taught for books, which is even greater than that contempt for books which distinguishes the wise. When he leafed through a catalogue, stood in front of the bookshop windows, sat in the quiet mildly dusty rooms of the library, regarded the dark-green backs of innumerable books on the tall wide shelves, the military ranks of green lampshades on the long tables, the deep devotion which makes every reader in the library look like a pious worshipper in a church, he was seized by the fear that he did not know the All-Important, and that one life might be too short to gain experience of it. He read and learned hastily, unsystematically, following changing inclinations, attracted by a title or a recollection of having heard of it before. He filled notebooks with observations that he took to be 'fundamental' and was almost inconsolable if a phrase, a date, a name escaped him. He listened to all lectures, necessary and unnecessary. He was always to be seen in the auditorium, always in the last row, which was also usually the highest. From there he overlooked the bent heads of the audience, the open white notebooks, the tiny blurred shorthand. The professor was so far away that to a certain extent he had lost his private humanity, was no more than a purveyor of knowledge. But Friedrich remained solitary, surrounded by candid faces in which nothing was evident but youth. One could, at a pinch, distinguish the races. Social differences were recognizable only by secondary characteristics. The well-to-do had manicured fingernails, tiepins, well-cut suits. All around a stone-deaf stolid wellbeing.

Only in the eyes of some Jewish students there shone a shrewd, a crafty or even a foolish melancholy. But it was the melancholy of blood and race, handed down to the individual and acquired by him without risk. In the same way, the others had inherited their wellbeing. Only groups distinguished themselves from each other by ribbons, colours, convictions. They prepared themselves for a barrack-room life and each already carried his rifle, his so-called 'Ideal'.

At that time we had a common acquaintance named Leopold Scheller, who happened to be the only student with whom Friedrich associated. He concealed nothing, always told the truth, naturally only the truth as he knew it, and put up with any insult that was flung at him. He did not believe it could be meant personally. If anyone offended his honour, as he saw it, by a look or a deliberate or chance shove in the Great Hall, it was not so much a matter of his honour, as that of the students' club to which he belonged. When Friedrich was bored he went to Scheller, who did not seem to be acquainted with boredom. He was always preoccupied with his philosophy of life.

He once surprised Friedrich with the information that he had got engaged. And he at once reached into his trouser-pocket, where he usually carried his pistol in a leather case. On this occasion he took out a wallet and out of the wallet a photograph. He noted Friedrich's amazement and said : 'My fiancée has taken my pistol away. She won't permit it.'

The photograph showed a pretty young woman of some eighteen years. She had black eyes and hair. 'She's certainly not a blonde then,' said Friedrich.

'She is Italian,' replied Scheller evenly, as if he had never been a Teuton.

'But,' persisted Friedrich, 'what are you doing with an Italian girl?'

'Love conquers all,' began Scheller. 'It is the greatest power on earth. Besides, I shall be making a German of her.'

'And how long have you known the lady?'

'Since the day before yesterday,' replied Scheller, beaming. 'I accosted her in the park.'

'And engaged already?'

'There's nothing else for it – either, or.'

'And your Club?'

'I'm resigning. Because she doesn't care for it. I wrote today to ask her father for her hand. He is a bank-clerk in Milan. My fiancée is with relatives here. We are getting married in two months' time. How do you like her?'

'Enormously!'

'Don't you agree? She is beautiful? She is unique?' And he laid a small piece of tissue-paper over the photograph and tucked it away again in his pistol pocket.

Although Friedrich did not consider Scheller's happiness lasting and feared disillusion for his friend, he nevertheless experienced in the proximity of this infatuation the warming reflection of a bliss not previously encountered, and he sunned himself in the other's love as if he lay in a strange meadow. Scheller was an entirely happy man. From lack of understanding he was incapable of a moment's doubt – a condition that normally accompanies love as shadow accompanies light. As the bliss he received was boundless, he radiated it again outwards. It was a bliss mightier than Scheller himself. Friedrich envied him and simultaneously relished the misery of his own solitude. He now imagined that his entire life would acquire meaning and expression when he met the woman he sought. Although he considered Scheller's method of picking up a girl in the park foolish, he did betake himself to the green spaces, which is not the colour of hope but of yearning. Moreover, everything was already autumnal and yellow. And the impatience of his searching heart waxed as the world approached winter.

35

He began to study with redoubled zeal. But as soon as he put down a book, it seemed to him as foolish as Scheller himself. Scholarship concealed what was really important as the rock strata concealed the earth's centre – secret, ever burning, ever invisible, not to be revealed before the end of the world. One learned about amputating legs, Gothic grammar, canon law. One could just as easily have learnt how to store furniture, manufacture wooden legs or pull teeth. And even philosophy made up its own answers and interpreted the sense of the question in relation to the answer that suited it. It was like a schoolboy who alters the problem set him to fit the false result of his mathematical labours.

Before long Friedrich began to become a less frequent attender in the lecture theatres. 'No,' he said, 'I'd rather pass the time with Grünhut. I have seen through them all. This intellectual flirtation of the elegant professors who lecture to the daughters of high society in the evenings from six to eight. A light-hearted excursion into philosophy, Renaissance art history, with lantern-slides in a darkened hall, national economy with sarcastic remarks about Marxism – no, that's not for me. And then, the so-called strict professors, who give lectures at a quarter past eight in the mornings, just after sunrise, so as to be free for the rest of the day – for their own work. The bearded senior lecturers who are on the look-out for a good marriage so that, through some connection with the Minister of Education, they may at last become established professors with salaries. And the malicious smiles of spiteful examiners, who carry off glorious victories over failed candidates. The University is an institution for the children of good middle-class homes with well-organized primary teaching, eight years of middle school, private coaching by tutors, the prospect of a judgeship, of a prosperous legal practice or a government office through marrying a second cousin – not a first cousin, because of consanguinity. And finally for the blockheads of the uniformed students' societies who fight each other, for pure Aryans, pure Zionists, pure Czechs, pure Serbs. Not for me! I'd rather write addresses with Grünhut.'

Once he discovered Savelli's name in one of the library catalogues. The book was entitled *International Capital and the Petroleum Industry.* He looked for the book and did not find it. It was out on loan. And as if this incident had been a sign from above he immediately betook himself from the library to Savelli.

In Savelli's room, on the fifth floor of a grey tenement in a proletarian district, there were three men. They had removed their jackets and hung them over the chairs they were sitting on. An electric bulb on a long flex hung from the ceiling and swung low over the rectangular table, constantly moved by the breath of the men talking but also by their repeated attempts to shift the lamp out of their field of vision whenever it hid one or the other. Sometimes, irritated by the annoying bulb but without recognizing it as the cause of his impatience, one of the three would get up, walk twice round the table, cast a searching glance at the sofa by the wall, and resume his original place. It was impossible just to sit down on the sofa. Heavy books and light newspapers, coloured pamphlets, prospectuses, dark-green library volumes, manuscripts and unused octavo sheets yellowing at the edges lay there higgledy-piggledy, and all subject to unknown laws which prevented the heavy volumes of an encyclopaedia from sliding off a thin stack of green pamphlets

37

Savelli had relinquished the chairs to his guests and sat on a pile of eight thick books, but still so low that his chin just projected above the table-top.

One of those present was powerful and broad-shouldered. He kept his large hairy fists on the table. His skull was round and bald, his eyebrows so thin and sparse as to be barely visible, his eyes small and bright, his mouth red and fleshy, his chin like a block of marble. He wore a red Russian blouse of some shiny material with a strong reflection, and no one could see him without at once thinking of an executioner. He was Comrade P., a Ukrainian, placid, even-tempered and trustworthy, and with a remarkable cunning which was hidden under his bulk like silver under the earth. Next to him sat Comrade T., a yellow-brown face with a black moustache and a wide black imperial, eyeglasses on his prominent nose, and dark eyes which seemed to betray a kind of restless hunger. Opposite him stood the momentarily empty chair of the third comrade. He was the most restless of them all and the frailty of his limbs, the pallor of his skin, justified his unease.

He had just been speaking when Friedrich entered and was now drumming with lean fingers on the dark window-pane as if telegraphing morse signals into the night. His face bore a modest thin nautical beard like a faded frame round a portrait. His eyes were hard and bright when he removed his spectacles. Behind them they looked thoughtful and wise. This was R., with whom Friedrich struck up a rapid friendship at the time, and whose enemy he was later to become.

The sentence which still rang in Friedrich's ears immediately revealed the speaker to him. 'I'll be hanged,' he had said, before at once correcting himself, 'that is,

38

they can hang me if we have a war within five years.'

Then there was silence for a time. Savelli got up, recognized Friedrich at once, and signed to him to sit where he liked. Friedrich looked round in vain and sat down cautiously on a pile of books on the sofa.

No one paid him any attention. P. stood up. His great bulk immediately darkened the room. He took up a stance behind the back of his chair and said : 'There's no other possibility. One of us has to go. The situation is so critical that we may all be for it overnight. Then the connection will be broken and the money lost over there for good. Berzejev is an officer, he has to look after his own interests. Desertion will be difficult for him. I have a direct report. He writes that he was jittery right through the manoeuvres. When he got back, Levicki was in Kiev, Gelber in Odessa. No one in Kharkov.'

'You'll have to go yourself,' interrupted Savelli.

'Make your will !' cried R.

'Comrade R. is nervous as usual,' said Savelli very softly.

'I don't deny it,' retorted R. smilingly, thereby displaying two rows of strikingly white and even teeth which no one would have suspected behind his narrow lips. The teeth emitted a fearsome gleam so that the sensitive peaceable nature of his face vanished and even his eyes became malicious.

'I've never claimed to be a hero and don't intend to risk my life. In any case, Savelli gives me no opportunity.'

They all laughed, except for the one with the dark hair. He shook his head, his pince-nez quivered and, as he gave the dangling lamp which now obstructed his view a shove so that it began to swing even more wildly, looking like a large irritated moth, he banged his other hand on the table and said resentfully : 'Don't be funny.'

When they broke up they shook Friedrich's hand, as if he were an old acquaintance.

'I saw you once on the Ring,' Savelli said to him. 'What are you doing now? Are you working? I don't mean studying.' He meant whether Friedrich was working for the Cause. Friedrich confessed that he was doing nothing. Savelli spoke of the war. It might break out within a week. The Russian General Staff was at work in Serbia. Russian agents trailed the émigrés in Paris, Berlin and Vienna. Suspicious customers had appeared several weeks ago in a café they frequented in the 9th precinct. Would Friedrich put in an appearance?

'I'll meet you again, here or at the café,' said Friedrich.

'Good-day!' said Savelli, as if he were taking leave of a man who had given him a light.

R. was without doubt the most interesting man besides P., Dr T., and Savelli. A number of younger men gathered round him and formed his 'group'. They walked through the late still nights. R. addressed them, they hung on his words.

'Tell me,' he began, 'whether this world isn't as quiet as a cemetery. People sleep in their beds like graves, they read a leading article, dunk a crisp croissant in their coffee, the whipped cream spills over the edge of the cup. Then they tap their egg carefully with the knife, out of respect for their own breakfast. The children saunter off to school with satchels and dangling blackboard sponges to learn about emperors and wars. The workers have already been at work in the factories for a long time, young girls glueing cartridges, big men cutting steel. For some hours, soldiers have been at exercise in the fields.

Trumpets blare. Meanwhile it's ten o'clock, councillors and ministers drive up to their offices, sign, sign, telegraph, dictate, telephone; typists sit in editorial offices and take dictation, pass it to editors who conceal and disclose, disguise and reveal. And as if nothing eventful had happened during the day, bells shrill to signal in the evening and the theatres fill with women, flowers and perfume. And then the world falls asleep again. But we are awake. We hear the ministers come and go, the kings and emperors groaning in their sleep, we hear how the steel is sharpened in the factories, we hear the birth of the big guns and the soft rustle of papers on the desks of diplomats. Already we see the great conflagration, from which men can no longer salvage their small sorrows and their small joys . . . .'

8

Friedrich now worked – as he and his friends tended to say – 'for the Cause'. He got himself into the habit of obtaining the enthusiasm, without which he could not live, from renunciation and anonymity. He even charmed a stimulus from the inexorability he had so feared, comfort from despair. He was young. And he believed not only in the efficacy of sacrifice, but also in the reward which engarlands sacrifice like flowers a grave. And yet there were hours, his 'weak' ones as he called them, in which he indulged a private hope that the Idea might triumph, and that he might live to experience it. But he owned to this only when he met R.

'Don't worry about that!' said R. 'I believe only in the altruism of the dead. We would all like to experience the right moment and a sweet revenge.'

'Except Savelli!' said Friedrich.

'You deceive yourself,' replied R., not without malevolence, or so it seemed to me at the time. 'You don't know Savelli. People will only understand him when it's too late. He acts the part of a man who no longer owns his heart because he has presented it to mankind. But don't be taken in, he has none. I prefer an egoist. Egoism is a sign of humanity. But our friend is not human. He has the temperament of a crocodile in the drought, the imagination of a groom, the idealism of an Izvoschik.'

'But what about all he's done so far?'

'A stupid error, to judge men by their deeds. Forget the bourgeois historians! Men get involved with affairs as innocently as they do with dreams. Our friend could just as well have organized pogroms as robbed banks!'

'Then why does he stay in our camp?'

'Because he's not talented enough, in our view, not versatile enough to free himself from the weight of his past. Men of his kind keep to their chosen path. He's no traitor. But he is our enemy. He hates us, as Russian peasants hate city intellectuals. He hates me in particular.'

'Why you in particular?'

'Because he has good cause to. Look at it properly. I'm no Russian. I'm a European. I know that I am separated from our comrades much more than most of us intellectuals are from the proletarians. I'm unlucky. I have a western education. Although I'm a radical, I like the centre. Although I prepare for the great uprising, I like moderation. I can't help myself.'

R. abandoned himself to the gusto of his formulation. And Friedrich copied him. Both began to outdo each other in contradictions. From both at that time one could hear a statement which was startling then and today sounds almost obvious: 'The Tsar is no gentleman, he's a bourgeois. He marks the beginning of the democratic era in Russia, the era of a democracy of small peasants – and you'll see, Savelli's friends will push on with the work. If the Tsar doesn't hang us, they will.'

It was as if R. had set out systematically to destroy Friedrich's fervour, his romantic enthusiasm for all the trappings of secret conspiracy. In R.'s company, even danger gained a ridiculous aspect. 'It's no lie,' he would say in the halls which stank of beer, pipe tobacco and sweat, 'that it's easier to die for the masses than to live with them.' Then he would step onto the platform, demand stronger support for the Party, threaten the ruling class, shout for blood, and cry: 'Long live the World Revolution!'

The police inspector would blow his whistle, the officers stormed into the hall, the meeting broke up. R. disappeared in a flash. He did not expose himself to the fists of the police.

It may well be that Friedrich would have taken another path if he had not become R.'s friend. For ultimately it was R. who instigated Friedrich to go to Russia, who aroused the younger man's ambition, the naïve ambition to demonstrate that one was not a 'fainthearted intellectual'. But there was also another factor.

I have the suspicion that Friedrich's voluntary journey to Russia, which ended ultimately in a compulsory spell

43

in Siberia, was the foolish outcome of a foolish infatuation which he took for hopeless at the time and whose importance he plainly exaggerated. But we have no right to enquire into the personal motives for an action that Friedrich wanted to carry out in the service of his Idea. We must content ourselves with a description of certain events.

9

He thought no more of the woman in the carriage – or he imagined that he had forgotten her. But one day, by chance, he saw her again – and he was startled. For it was like an encounter with a picture come to life which had been left in store in a particular room in a particular museum, or an encounter with a forgotten idea which has remained in a deep and hidden region of the memory. He no longer remembered who she was when she asked him in a corridor at the University where Lecture Theatre 24 was. He only recognized her after she had disappeared. Like a distant star, she had occupied a few seconds in impinging on his retina. He followed her. In the darkened room someone was reading aloud about some painter or other, someone was showing various lantern-slides, and the darkness was like a second smaller room within the hall. It enclosed both her and him with equal density.

He waited. He did not hear a single word or see a single

picture. He saw that the door opened, and that she left the hall.

He followed her at a distance which seemed to be ordained and laid down by adoration. He was afraid that a side-street might swallow her, a carriage bear her away, an acquaintance await her. His tender gaze seized the distant brown shimmer of her profile between the edge of her fur collar and her dark hat. The regular rhythm of her steps imparted gentle wavy movements to the soft material of her jacket, to her hips and back. She stopped in front of a small shop in a quiet side-street and laid a hesitant, pensive hand on the door-handle. She went in. He came nearer. He looked through the window. She was sitting at the table, face turned towards him, trying on gloves. She was leaning on her left hand, her fingers were outspread in patient expectation. She slipped on the new leather, closed her hand into a fist and opened it again, stroked the left hand caressingly with the right, and unfolded joints and fingers in attractive and absorbing play.

She left the shop. He had no time to move away. Her first glance fell on him and, as he involuntarily removed his hat, she stood there as if she intended to acknowledge him, as if she was considering whether she should assume the indifferent smile suited to acquaintances one has forgotten. Eventually, as he made no move, she turned to go. He came a step closer. She was visibly embarrassed. The urge to fly seized him together with the fear of ridicule. The awareness that he must say something the very next moment was surpassed by the silent avowal that he could think of nothing to say. The soft oval of her brown face confused him by its proximity, like her startled dark gaze and the delicate bluish skin of her eyelids, and even the small parcel she held in her hand. 'If only she

45

didn't continue to smile,' he thought. 'I must make it clear to her at once that I am not one of her acquaintances.' So, hat in hand, he said : 'I can't help it if you're alarmed. The situation was too much for me. I followed you unintentionally. You left the shop before I expected. I accosted you without knowing you. I have therefore misled you without intending to do so. Please forgive me.'

As he was speaking he was surprised by the calmness and precision of his words. Her smile vanished and reappeared. It was like a light that comes and goes.

'I quite understand,' she said.

Friedrich bowed, she likewise attempted an acknowledgment, and both laughed.

He was surprised to find that she was not married. He could not understand now why he had taken her for a married woman. Also, it was not her carriage in which she had been travelling that August day. The carriage belonged to her friend, Frau G., to whom she had been invited. Was she a student? No, she only attended the lectures of Professor D., who was a family friend. Her father, as is the way of some old gentlemen, did not permit her to study. She would certainly have had her way if her mother had been alive. Her mother would have been helpful. And a transient sadness passed over her face.

She stood in front of a cab-rank, she was due at the theatre, she had an appointment. Already Friedrich saw a coachman jump down from his box and strip the blankets from the back of his horse.

'I should very much like to come with you, if you've the time,' said Friedrich quickly.

She laughed. He was embarrassed. 'Let's go then,' she said, 'but right away.'

Now it was done he could no longer speak calmly. The

talk was only on neutral topics, the hard winter and Professor D., the tedious public and private balls, the meanness of rich people and the poor street lighting. She vanished into the theatre.

He abandoned himself to an animated aimlessness, a sort of holiday. He entered the foyer in which she had disappeared. It was a quarter of an hour before the start of the performance. One heard the carriages driving up, the horses' solemn neighing, the clatter of their hoof-beats and the murmured exhortations of the coachmen. The foyer wafted an odour of perfume, powder, clothes, a confusion of greetings. Many men were waiting there, leaning against the walls, removing their hats, bowing more or less deeply, only bowing or smiling while bowing. He could deduce the status of those who entered from the mien and attitude of those who awaited them. The people stood in their corners like living mirrors. But they themselves also had rank and character and were repeatedly confirmed in the position they held in the world by the response they received. The beautiful women seemed to see no one; nevertheless they scanned all those present with the alert and unobtrusive gaze with which commanders inspect regiments ready to march one last time before the General arrives. None of those present escaped these beautiful women. They did not overlook even the doorman or the policeman. Their eyes scattered rapid questions and received slow and languishing answers. Officers in every shade of blue and brown, all in gleaming patent leather boots and narrow black trousers, spread an amiable cadence of sound and a harmless motley of colour. For the first time Friedrich felt no hatred toward them and even a certain solidarity with the policeman, who was to be thanked because the harmony of this

47

elegant turmoil was undisturbed by drunkards or crimi-
nals. 'No one here suspects what I am,' he thought. 'They
take me for a little student.' When a woman's gaze rested
on him, he felt gratitude towards the entire sex. 'These
creatures have instinct,' he told himself. 'The men are
coarse.' Suddenly he pitied these society ladies. They
mourned away their lives, their beauty wilted, at the side
of boorish lieutenants and brutish moneylenders. They
needed quite different men. Naturally, he thought of
himself.

A shrill bell rang through the house like a joyous
alarm. People's movements quickened, the hubbub grew
louder. The doors flew open and three minutes later the
foyer was empty. The policeman sat down on an empty
chair in the corner. The box-office window was slammed
to from within by an invisible hand. The silvery arc-lights
in front of the entrance went out. The performance had
ended in the foyer, another was just beginning on the
stage. The coachmen came inside, little men who looked
like postmen out of uniform. They gathered round the
doorman and parleyed with him. They were sub-agents
and fly-by-night ticket touts. The policeman turned away
so as not to have to see them. In the foyer there was no
longer any fragrance of women's perfume. These poor
folk diffused an aroma of goulash, old clothes and rain. It
was as if the poor now gathered in the foyer stood, like
the figures in a weather-house, at the opposite end of the
same gang-plank to which the rich too were nailed, and
as if fixed rules governed the appearance, now of the
fortunate, and now of the wretched.

Friedrich left the theatre. It was time to seek out his
friends in the café. But on this particular day he would
rather not have seen them. He felt embarrassed before

them. 'They are bound to see,' he told himself, 'that I am in love. R. will immediately unmask me as a "romantic", a description which, in his mouth, sounds like the word "parricide".' No, he could not meet the comrades. Savelli, for instance, did not fall in love, Comrade T. loved only the Revolution. The Ukrainian had subjected his entire colossal bulk to the Idea as one subjects a race to a master. And as for R., he obviously denied the possibilities of love. Only he, Friedrich, had room in his breast for renunciation and ambition, revolution and infatuation.

There was nothing left for him to do but to climb the poorly-lit stairs to Grünhut, for he could not remain alone. He smelled the stink of the cats which rushed helter-skelter away from him in inexplicable panic, heard the voices from behind the doors ranked closely in the corridors, numbered as in hotels. The midwife's door bore the notice: 'Knock loudly, bell out of order.' He heard Grünhut's light step.

'Long time no see,' said Grünhut. And immediately after: 'Psst, there's clients inside.'

He was writing his addresses. He could now easily manage up to 400 a day. Was Friedrich writing still? No, he was working now, still had enough money for two months, and intended to find something else soon.

Grünhut now resumed his old complaints against the world. As always he returned in the end to the question: 'What do you think of an anonymous letter to the man I told you about?'

He didn't want Friedrich's advice, he was thinking of writing an unusual sort of letter, by two hands, each word written alternately. He already knew the attested experts. In any complicated case they were at a loss. A second person must be involved, and not just on account of the

49

handwriting. It might be necessary to arrange a rendez-vous. Still, in Grünhut's opinion two would so confuse anonymity that no one would know what was going on.

Friedrich's opposition pained him. His unshakable belief in the young man's criminal nature was transformed into an injured respect for the youth who, in Grünhut's opinion, was probably planning far more important and profitable crimes.

Various noises emerged from the midwife's room. Water, words murmured in a woman's deep voice, a chair pushed back, a metal object in contact with glass and wood.

'Do you hear that?' said the little man. 'On a spring evening, in a private room in a hotel, you hear very different things. Nightingales sing, a gipsy plays the violin, champagne corks pop. Where are they now, the nightingales? Frau Tarka hinted to me who it is in there. The wife of a professor, because of an affair with a sculptor. What's more, a good friend of mine. Put some business my way. An extremely productive man, thinks himself as irresistible as any blackguard. Frau Tarka has to thank sculptors and painters for most of her little jobs.

'People have their portraits painted so much nowadays. They live it up in the studios. Do you think a woman can resist a studio? Such lovely disorder under the blue sky, high up on the top floor where only God peers in through the glass roof. You lie there and look up. You see the white clouds passing, interspersed by flocks of birds, and you yearn and yearn again. A canvas in the corner, a witness that another woman was once naked here. And the painter goes on talking. Everything he knows he has acquired from pornographic works and erotic books. His eye lusts after contour and sticks to the surface. "What a line, dear lady," he says, "connects your neck with the swell of your breast!" Believe me, if a lieutenant said that it would be an insult and the husband would shoot it out with him in the woods at dawn. When a painter says it, it's an artistic judgment. These so-called connoisseurs aren't paying compliments, they're merely making technical appraisals. They apply these to the entire body. "What a provocative thigh!" they say, palette in hand. Some talk about the Renaissance. The sculptor B., for instance, who comes to visit Madame here from time to time, I often have a little chat with him. That is, he does the chatting. Nothing but false rubbish from the erotic books. Gives me an order once. Pornographic engravings; because I happen to know a bookseller, I have to go and make the purchase. He still owes me my commission and the bookseller his money. The bookseller goes along, makes a fuss. "Come tomorrow," says the Master. Next day, he smilingly gives him the book back. Then he tells me, a few weeks later, he only wanted the pictures for just that one afternoon, for a girl from a good family. And all I did was to undo a blouse. Because I'm no artist. Plain as a pikestaff, the way things have changed. We've already had the question of art. The emancipation of women, too. Notice how the two connect? So-called family ties are loosening. The daughters of the privy councillors have their portraits painted and study German philology. And, as for what I did – of course it was many years ago – nowadays you get respect for that kind of thing. My public prosecutor is still alive. He'll never see another such indictment. My defence counsel even in those days supported the theory of demonic possession. He talked nonsense about irresistible urges, heredity and so on. Fair is fair. My father was an

51

inoffensive man, he ran an exchange-office, had serious worries and not the slightest interest in morality.'

It grew quiet in the next room, a door opened, a key rattled. Grünhut detained Friedrich a few minutes longer.

'Until they've gone downstairs,' he said. 'I don't want any indiscretions.'

10

As, in accordance with the promise he had given his dying wife, he could not marry again, but could not live without a woman and did not want his child to become acquainted with the habits of a lusty widower, Herr Ludwig von Maerker, then still departmental head in a ministry, decided to send his daughter to a children's home and later to a girls' boarding school where she would be brought up together with orphans of the same social standing. Therefore, after he had disposed of Hilde, he engaged a housekeeper but took her only to the circus and music-halls. The theatres remained closed to her. She called this an injustice and so granted herself the right to embitter Herr von Maerker's life and make increasing demands in the house. She controlled his every step and every outlay. And whenever he complained about the restriction of his liberty, she replied with that bitter sarcasm which can herald a fainting-fit as well as an apoplexy: 'So I can't have this little entitlement? I, a woman whom you don't even take to the theatre?' Once a year Herr von Maerker escaped from the housekeeper. He travelled to Switzerland to visit his daughter. She grew too tall for him, was soon a teenager. He found her beautiful and regretted, in his most private moments, that he was her father and not her seducer. But she had been seduced long before by her own fantasies. Although Herr von Maerker had read a number of French novels about nunneries and girls' boarding schools, he believed – like most men – in the depravity of all women except his nearest and dearest. Lack of principle begins only with cousins. A good deal was said about the prospect of having Hilde back at home again soon. And, before he was aware of it, Herr von Maerker was going grey at the temples, his housekeeper grew old and wrinkled, her hopes of marriage to her friend and the prospect of a joint box at the theatre vanished, Hilde blossomed – as they say – into a young woman, returned to her father's house and began to lead her own life.

The times were strongly in favour of freedom for the female sex; not so Herr von Maerker, who had meanwhile become permanent head of a ministerial department and was therefore well aware of the lack of masculine freedom. His daughter's opinions made him feel half embittered and half ashamed at belonging to the previous generation, for men feel shame at becoming old as if it were a secret vice. He retreated silently before his daughter's vigorous offensive. He suffered and even gradually became wise. He belonged to that breed of average men who acquire understanding only in later years because they have had to keep silent for so long, and for whom nothing remains but to become meditative. When Hilde, on behalf of all the daughters of the world, exclaimed: 'Our mothers were exploited and betrayed!' Herr von Maerker felt it as a calumny on his dead wife and an insult by his daughter. He wondered where Hilde had acquired so much robust callousness and shocking rhetoric. He still knew nothing about his daughter.

She was no different from the young women of her time and station. She transformed the submissive romanticism of her mother into an Amazon martiality, demanded the recognition of civil rights, including, in passing as it were, free love. Under the slogan 'Equal rights for all!' the daughters of good homes at that period rushed into life, into the high schools, into railway trains, luxury liners, into the dissecting-room and the laboratory. For them there blew through the world that familiar fresh breeze that every new generation believes it has discovered. Hilde was determined not to surrender herself in marriage. Her 'closest friend' had committed the betrayal of marrying the enormously wealthy Herr G.; she owned carriages, horses, flunkeys, coachmen, liveries. But Hilde, who gladly enjoyed sharing in her friend's wealth and laid claim to the carriages and the liveries for shopping expeditions, asserted : 'Irene's happiness means nothing to me, she has sold her freedom.' The men to whom she said this found her charming, unusually intelligent, delightfully self-willed. And as, on top of this, she had a dowry and a father with good connections, one or the other thought of marrying her despite her principled objection, in their old-fashioned masculine way.

Her father would only have given her to certain of her acquaintances. Certainly not to everyone of those with whom she associated, less out of interest than from the need to demonstrate her independence. She formed a so-called circle. Through her father she knew some hopeful young officials and officers, through Professor D., a few lecturers and students of art history. Through her rich married friend, whose husband fancied himself a Maecenas, a composer, two painters, a sculptor and three writers.

All these young people, none of whom suspected that they would soon be decimated in a world war, behaved as if they had to burst out of never-ending bondage. The young officials spoke of the dangers which threatened the old Empire, of the necessity for far-reaching national autonomy or a strong centralizing grip, of the dissolution of Parliament, a careful choice of ministers, a break with Germany, a rapprochement with France, or else an even closer tie with Germany and a challenge to Serbia. Some wanted to avoid war, others to provoke it; both thought that it would be a question of only a lighthearted little war. The young officers held slow promotion and the stupidity of the general staff responsible for everything. The lecturers, meek as young theologians, concealed under their store of knowledge a hunger for position and dowries. The artists let it be understood that they had a direct line to Heaven, derided authority, simultaneously championed Olympus, the café and the studio. Each was audacious, and yet each was really rebelling only against his own father. Hilde regarded each as a personality and at the same time as a good comrade. She believed she was maintaining pure friendship, but if anyone failed to pay her a compliment, she began to doubt his personality. To be sure, she had no time for outmoded love but she broke off relationships with any man who did not give her to understand that he was in love with her.

She listed her encounter with Friedrich under her 'notable experiences'. His obvious poverty was a novel feature in her circle of acquaintances. His far-reaching

55

radicalism marked him off from the minor rebels. Nevertheless, she was a little excited the next time she went to the lecture.

'Perhaps I might come with you,' he said. Naturally, she thought, but merely said : 'If it amuses you.' And, as it was raining, she imagined that she would go with him to his room or a café. 'But perhaps he's no money,' she mused, and from then on no longer registered what he said. Outside in the street, where the wet, the wind and the showers threw people into confusion, he endeavoured several times to take her by the arm. Her arm anticipated his hand. It will be obvious how slight an effect emancipation had actually had on Hilde.

They reached the little café where he was a regular customer, and where he could owe or borrow money without embarrassment. As if it had only just occurred to him, he said : 'We're wet, come along in.' She felt the faint intimation of happiness a young woman feels when her lover guides her into a room.

They were sitting in the corner. 'He is a regular customer and at home here,' she concluded rapidly, and had already made up her mind to surprise him there from time to time. At times their hands touched on the table-top, quickly withdrew from each other, and independently experienced embarrassment, yearning, curiosity, as if they had their own hearts. Her sleeve rubbed against him. Their feet touched. Their plates clashed, became alive. Every movement one of them made conveyed a hidden meaning to the other. He loved her bracelet as much as her fingers, her narrow sleeve as well as her arm. He asked her about her mother because he wanted to see her looking sad again. But she did not. She merely described the photograph she had of the dead woman and promised to show it to him. The time at boarding-school, he thought, would have been strict and dreary. She recalled the secret nightly talks that she had long forgotten, comfortably included in the category of 'childish behaviour'. Recollections distressed her. She yearned for one of his casual and startled contacts. She wanted to grasp his hand and blushed. She recalled some painter's unambiguous importunity and now transferred this to Friedrich. His remarks made her impatient, but at the same time she thought : 'He is intelligent and remarkable.'

'It's late,' she said. 'I must go home.'

He had been on the point of telling her about the goings-on at the midwife's as an illustration of the decadence of society, a symptom of its decline. She propitiated him with a smile. He consoled himself with the length of the walk. Once outside, she began to talk of her youth. It was dark. The street-lamps burned dimly, sparse and damp. The walls seemed to cast double shadows. Suddenly she took his arm as if to tell him more. 'Maybe he'll ask,' she thought. But he did not ask. She began :

'At night-time we used to sleep four in a large room, one in each corner. My bed was on the left, by the window. Opposite me slept little Gerb. Her father was a German finance official, from Hessen, I think. In the night she got into my bed. We were sixteen then. She told me that her cousin, a military cadet, had explained everything to her, as it were. That's frightful, isn't it?'

Friedrich did not understand what she wanted to be asked. 'I think,' he said, 'that you wouldn't have found it so frightful if you had realized that sixty per cent of all working-class children between twelve and sixteen are no longer virgins. Have you any idea what it's like in the

57

tenements?' His old rage! He resumed with a bitter zeal and took away all her appetite for confidences. In a good boarding school, where only four girls slept in a room, one could have no idea of a worker's dwelling. He described one to her. He explained what it was like not to have a bed of one's own, a casual ward, the life of the exiles and the politically condemned.

She comforted herself. 'What strange company!' she thought arrogantly. She asked him about his youth. He told her about his activities on the frontier. 'I envy you,' she said. 'You are free and strong. Will you call on me? Wednesday afternoon?'

Her smile illuminated the dark hall like a light.

Most young men seemed to her as tedious as her father. She longed to be a man and despised men who did nothing with their masculinity. She would have had Friedrich suave like the lieutenant and importunate like the painter, and for the first time in many years she cried in bed, naked and abandoned to the darkness, a poor girl without a trace of emancipation.

In the morning she reviewed the week's programme with the vague intent of reforming her life. It was Sunday. The seamstress came on Monday, Tuesday she was going with Frau G. to the theatre, guests on Wednesday, lecture on Thursday, her aunt on Friday, Saturday two gentlemen from the Ministry for dinner and an hour's sitting for the portrait-painter in the afternoon. She wanted to invite Frau G. to accompany her, but her friend had no time, she had to make a long-planned excursion with her husband to his relatives, three hours in the train. Within the next five minutes she forgot about the excursion, looked in the paper to see what performances there were on Saturday, blushed, became confused, and turned quickly to another topic. For the first time there was an element of hostility in her farewell, and neither the deliberately hearty handshake nor the customary embrace, which this time even lasted some seconds longer than usual, had quite the power to erase it. 'She regards me as her rival,' Hilde reflected quickly. Her 'best friend'.

She went into the little café in order to surprise Friedrich, did not find him, and left an invitation for Saturday afternoon.

He came and met the painter. He already knew this striking man by sight. He detested the prominent overweening skull, the broad white forehead, the bushy eyebrows which their owner seemed to water daily like cultivated fields. They overshadowed his empty eyes in such a way that their dark depths appeared like enigmatic oceans. He detested the high, soft and contrived casual collar, from which emerged a massive double chin as if to support the chin itself. He detested so-called 'fine heads' in general. They employed a great part of their energy in appearing even more important than nature had intended, and it was as if they had transferred their talents to the mirror when they got up every morning.

Hilde gave the painter preference. She was annoyed with Friedrich because she had had a bad night on his account. She blamed him for appearing different on a gloomy rainy evening than on a bright afternoon. Moreover, he was now sullen and silent. He watched while the painter produced ten sketches in the course of half an hour with flying fingers and a menacing gaze which jumped from Hilde to the paper and back again. Hilde was restive. Although her features seemed to remain unchanged, sudden transformations took place beneath

59

her skin and beneath her features, and only in her eyes was it possible to see how a light was extinguished and then rekindled.

Friedrich's silence caused the painter to lose his self-control. 'I must have you alone,' he said softly, as if to make it plain to Friedrich that the remark referred to a private matter. Friedrich got up, the painter cast his eyes up at the ceiling. He had the ability to see the world with his eyebrows rather than his eyes. He collected his sheets together with hasty resignation. As Hilde feared that he might be offended, she begged him to stay. But she allowed Friedrich to leave and he departed, silent and sullen, with the resolve to write her a meaningful letter to make it clear that she was leading an unworthy and untruthful life, that she would have to change, that she must break with this bourgeois behaviour and this mock rebellion.

He wrote all this hurriedly, as a man does who wants to save himself from an imminent danger. As he reached the fourth side, he reflected. He wanted to destroy the letter, but he recalled that, in all the books, there were lovers who tore up letters. On no account did he wish to appear ridiculous. And he quickly posted the letter.

R. came to his table. 'Been in love long? So it's true you've fallen in love, nothing to be ashamed of. It's a drive, like health, but just as one shouldn't use health to become even healthier, so you shouldn't feed love with your love. Sublimate it. Put it to good use. Otherwise it's trash.'

There was a pamphlet to translate into Italian. In a week it was May Day. Meetings. Having to be here and there. Saying a few words. P. threatened with expulsion. Savelli asked after Friedrich.

'Yes, yes,' said Friedrich, 'I'll make a start right away.'
He set to work. It was not really love that he could
convert into action, at most the productive melancholy of
the infatuated.

One evening, while he was writing, Hilde came into
the café. He pretended indifference, to her and even to
himself. She was not to believe that he was a bourgeois
portrait-painter. No, he had to work for the world's
salvation. No small thing. He experienced a malicious
triumph that she had brought her youth, her elegance,
her beauty into the small grey room.

She sat helplessly beside him, his long letter in her
hand. She had intended to discuss every sentence with
him. He begged her to wait, he had an article to write.
It's explosive, he thought, stimulated by the prospect of
reading it aloud to her if she begged him. She waited. He
had finished. It did not occur to her to ask. She was
thinking only of the letter. Almost meekly she began : 'I
brought the letter with me.' Her meekness irritated him.
'I beg your pardon,' he said, 'I wrote that letter in a crazy
mood. Don't think of it any more as a letter addressed
to you.'

She was still holding the paper in her hand. He seized
it and began to tear it up. She would have liked to grasp
his hand and was embarrassed. Her eyes filled with hot
tears. 'I'm crying again,' she thought, angered by her
relapse into an outdated past.

It was only a little moment, he did not look at her.
Convincingly, he played a hard arrogant part and his
hands tore up the letter mechanically. Now it was fifty
scraps of paper. They lay like small white corpses on the
dark marble slab. The waiter came, swept them with one
hand into the other and took them away.

'Buried,' she thought.

He wanted to say something conciliatory. Nothing conciliatory came. Over both of them there already reigned the eternal decree that governs misunderstandings between the sexes.

Now she was on her feet again, a stranger from another world in this café. He saw her once more through the window as she passed. And he did not realize that only a pane of glass separated her from him. He felt as if there were no chance, ever again, of leaving this café. As if, at this moment, the door had been walled up and his place were here, at this table, for eternity. He did not stir. Five minutes later he stepped outside. She was no longer to be seen.

II

From then on he thought about undertaking 'a long and dangerous journey'. An unaccountable sadness accompanied his work, endowed his efforts with a golden warmth and his voice with a melancholy resonance, and drew the first sharp furrows on his countenance. He seemed to have become taciturn. His bright gaze came from a remote distance and fixed itself on a remote objective. He wanted to go away and never return.

'I'm a poor man,' he once said to R., 'on the side of the poor. The world is not kind to me, I shall not be kind to it. It is full of injustice. I suffer from this injustice. Its capriciousness afflicts me. I want to afflict the mighty.'

'If I wanted to be fair, like Savelli for instance,' answered R., 'I should tell you that your place is with the saints of the Catholic Church and not with the anonymous heroes of the Party. I've discussed you with T. We are both of the opinion that, in the strict sense of the word, you are unreliable. If you are personally disillusioned, you want to hang the ministers. You belong to the eternal European intellectuals. Just now you are in sympathy with the proletariat, with whom you associate. But wait a bit, one day you'll see the open hatred of the human scum shining in the sad eyes of the young men whom you now lecture. Has that ever occurred to you? Whenever a working-man shakes my hand, it occurs to me that one day his hand might strike me as mercilessly as the hand of a policeman. Your outlook is false, it's the same as my own, that is why I can tell you this and that is why you can believe me. We might more usefully recognize that the poor are no better than the rich, the weak no nobler than the strong, and that, on the contrary, there must be power before there can be goodness.'

'I am going away,' said Friedrich.

'Quite right,' replied R. 'You must expose yourself to danger. Go to Russia. Take the risk of ending up in Siberia. T. has been there, K. was there, I was there. Get to know the strongest and stupidest proletariat in the world. You will find that it has in no way attained nobility through suffering. It's cruel of me to have to give a young man this advice, but you will find yourself cured of all illusions. Every one. And you won't ever fall in love again, to give just one example.'

He began his next lecture with the information that he had decided to go away, that someone else would take his

63

place. He glimpsed Hilde in one of the back rows in a deliberately unpretentious coat. What a masquerade, he thought angrily. He felt responsible for her presence. He felt it as a betrayal committed against those he was addressing. He began to read out the leading article of a bourgeois newspaper. It was an account of the determination of the Central Powers to safeguard the peace of the world, and of the strivings of this very world towards the conflagration of war. He produced a Russian, a French, an English newspaper and demonstrated to his audience that they all wrote the same. The lamp hung low over the lectern at which he stood and dazzled him. When he wanted to survey the small room, he saw the walls as a grey obscurity. They lost their solidity. They receded even further, like veils dispersed by the ring of his words. The faces that shone towards him out of the darkness multiplied tenfold. He listened attentively to his own voice, the ringing resonance of his speech. He stood there as if on the verge of a darkling sea. His best words were derived from the expectancy of his listeners. It seemed to him as if he spoke and listened at the same time, as if he said things and at the same time suffered things to be said to him, as if he were resonant and simultaneously heard the resonance.

There was a moment's quietness. The quietness was an answer. It sanctioned his authority like a seal of silence.

When he got down from the platform, Hilde had disappeared. He was annoyed at having looked for her. A few persons pressed his hand and wished him a good journey.

12

His departure was fixed for the evening of the following day. He still had over twenty-four hours to wait. Savelli had provided him with money, letters and commissions. He was to report first to Frau K. and stay with her. To return at the first safe available opportunity with part of the money, which was urgently needed here. He had a trunk full of newspapers. They were stuffed in the pockets, the sleeves, the linings of strange clothing with which he had been provided.

He was not afraid. He was pervaded by a current of peace, like a dying man conscious of a long and righteous life behind him. He could perish, nameless, forgotten, but not without trace. A drop in the ocean of the Revolution.

'I have taken a cordial farewell from R.,' he told me. 'R., whom everyone calls treacherous, whom no one can really tolerate, knows more than the others. He does not forget the infirmity of men where sentiment is concerned. He is aware of the hidden diversity of which we are all made up. No one trusts him entirely because he is many-sided. But, beyond that, he doesn't even trust himself, his incorruptible intelligence.'

He went to say goodbye to Grünhut.

'Where are you off to?'

There was silence for a few moments. Grünhut went to the window. It was as if he looked, not at the street, but only in the windowpane which had ceased to be transparent.

'What's got into you?' Grünhut cried in a tearful voice. 'I don't ask the reason for your journey, that I can guess. But why you?'

'I'm not even sure myself.'

Back to the windowpane.

'I'm seeing him for the last time,' thought Friedrich. His thoughts, which he had already directed towards death, suddenly made a volte-face.

'You don't realize, you don't realize,' said Grünhut. 'You're young. Do you really imagine that you will ever again be in a position to say : "I'm going far away"? Do you think life is endless? It's short, and has a few miserable possibilities to offer, and you must know how to cherish them. You can say "I want" twice, "I love" once, "I shall" twice, "I'm dying" once. That's all. Look at me. I'm certainly no one to envy. But I don't wish to die. I can probably still say once more 'I want" or "I shall". No great expectations at present but I can wait. I intend to suffer for nothing and for nobody. The tiny pain you feel when you prick your finger is considerable in relation to the shortness of your life. Yes, and to think that there are folk who let their hands be chopped off and their eyes put out for an idea, for an idea! For Humanity, in the name of Freedom! It's frightful!

'I understand well enough, you can't go back on this. One commits some act or other, one simply has to do it. Then we are held responsible, we are given a medal for a so-called heroic deed, we are thrown in jail for a so-called crime. We aren't responsible for anything. At most, we're responsible for what we *don't* do. If we were held responsible on *that* account, we'd be beaten up a hundred times a day and lie in jail a hundred times and be hanged a hundred times.'

He returned to the windowpane. And, his back turned to Friedrich, said quite gently : 'Go then, and see you come back. I've seen many go before now.'

Voices were suddenly audible in Frau Tarka's room next-door.

'Quiet,' whispered Grünhut, 'sit quite still where you are. A new client. The painter was here yesterday. I thought then that someone might be coming today. Won't stay long. First consultation. Stay here till she's gone.'

Soon they heard the door. 'Quick, before Madame comes in,' said Grünhut. A fleeting handshake, as if Grünhut had forgotten that it was farewell for ever.

13

Two days later he was sitting with old Parthagener at the inn 'The Ball and Chain'. It had not changed. Kapturak still continued to bring in deserters. Folk drank schnapps and ate salted peas. The rebels met at Chaikin's. The jurist still hoped to become a Deputy.

Kapturak arrived next morning. 'So you've not become a district commissioner? Yes, we're leaving already. The trunks I'll take with me. Expect them at the border tavern.' It was a holiday, the frontier officials were already sitting with the deserting soldiers, drinking and singing. Behind the counter stood the landlord, open-mouthed and goggle-eyed.

Friedrich stepped outside. The moist stars twinkled. A soft wind blew. One scented the wide plains from which it came.

A small tubby man with a black goatee suddenly stood next to Friedrich.

'A fine night,' he said, 'isn't it?'

'Yes,' said Friedrich, 'a fine night.'

'I'm arresting you, my dear Kargan,' said the man amiably. He had a chubby, white, almost feminine hand and short fingers. 'Get going!' he ordered.

Two men who suddenly came into view took Friedrich between them.

He felt only the wind, like a consolation from infinite space.

Book Two

It was evening. The water splashed softly and caressingly against the steamer floating on the Volga. The heavy regular thump of the engines could be heard between decks. The swaying lanterns cast light and shadow over the two hundred men who had lain down there, each exactly where he happened to have been standing when he set foot on the ship. At the quiet way-stations the engines fell silent and one heard the low shouts of sailors and porters and the slap of water against wood.

Most of the prisoners lay stretched out on the deck. A hundred and twenty of the two hundred between-deck passengers were in irons. They wore chains at their right wrist and right ankle. Those who were not fettered seemed almost like free men beside the chained men. Now and again there appeared a policeman, an inquisitive sailor. The prisoners took no notice either of their guards or their visitors. Although it was quite early in the evening and food was due to be handed out in half an hour, most slept, tired after the long march they had covered. The government was sending them on the slow cheap route by water, after having made them go a long distance on foot. The day after tomorrow they were to be freighted on the railroad. They were stocking up well on sleep.

Some of them already knew their way around. It was not the first time they had made this trip. These were experienced, settled down in a practical manner, and gave advice to the novices. They enjoyed a certain authority among their comrades. With the gendarmes they were linked by a kind of intimate hostility.

They were called to meals as if to an execution. They lined up behind one another, chains clanking between them. It seemed as if they were all strung on a single chain. A spoon landed with a regular splashing stroke in the cauldron, then there was the soft gurgle of a stream of soup flowing softly downwards, a damp mass fell on a hard metal plate. Heavy feet shuffled, a chain dragged clanking, and ever and again another detached himself from the line as if he had been unstrung. The lower space became filled with the vapour rising from two hundred metal plates and mouths. All ate. And, although they themselves conducted the spoon to their lips, it seemed as if they were being fed by alien arms which did not belong to their bodies. Their eyes, which were sated much sooner than their stomachs, already had the vacant look of repletion which characterizes the head of a family at table, the look that is already advancing into the domain of sleep.

'When I look at these men as they feed,' said Friedrich to Berzejev, a former lieutenant, 'I am convinced that they need nothing more than a ball and chain on the leg, a spoon in the right hand, and a tin plate in the left. The heart is so near the bowels, tongue and teeth so closely adjacent to the brain, the hands that write down thoughts can so easily slaughter a lamb and turn a spit, that I find myself as much at a loss before human beings as before a legendary dragon.'

'You talk like a poet,' replied Berzejev, smiled, and showed in his black beard two rows of gleaming teeth which seemed to confirm Friedrich's conjecture. 'I cannot find such words. But I too have seen that man is a puzzle, and above all that it is not possible to help him.'

Both felt alarmed. Were they not here because they wanted to help him? They turned away from each other.

'Good night,' said Berzejev.

Outside the guard was relieved.

2

After four days they were disembarked, led into a large room and entrained. They were refreshed as they trod solid ground again, and their chains gave a livelier ring. Even beneath the turning wheels of the train they felt the earth. Through the barred windows they saw grass and fields, cows and herdsmen, birches and peasants, churches and blue smoke over chimneystacks, the entire world from which they were cut off. And yet, it was a consolation that it had not perished, that it had not even altered. As long as houses stood and cattle grazed, the world awaited the return of the prisoners. Freedom was not like a possession which each one of them had lost. It was an element like the air.

Rumours circulated through the waggons. In recollection of the tidings heard and exchanged in recent prisons, they were called 'latrine reports'. Some said that the entire transport would go straight to Vierchoiansk, which was denounced by the knowledgeable as nonsense. Adrassionov, the NCO, had told one of the old hands whom

73

he was now transporting for the second time, that they would be taken to Tiumen, to one of the biggest prisons, the Tiuremni Zamok, or central prison for exiles. The experienced, who had already been there, began to depict the horrors of this jail. At first they shuddered at their own words and made their listeners shudder. But gradually, during their narration, the thrill they derived from their narrative exceeded its content, and the curiosity of the listeners dominated their terror. They sat there like children listening to stories of glass palaces. Panfilov and Sjemienuta, two old white-bearded Ukrainians, even described the solitary cells with a kind of nostalgia; and, so forgetful is the human heart and because the journey still seemed unending and its destination still uncertain despite the affirmations of the old hands, all of them believed for a few short hours that it was not they themselves but quite other strangers who were travelling towards the miseries of the prisons.

Friedrich and Berzejev resolved to stay together as far as possible. Berzejev had money. He knew how to bribe, swap lists and names and – while the other 'politicals' discussed the peasants, anarchy, Bakunin, Marx and the Jews – calculated whom he should give a cigarette and whom a rouble.

Although they travelled slowly, waited for hours at goods stations, the railway journey nevertheless seemed shorter than they had expected. Once again the chains rattled, once again there was a roll-call. They stood at the last station and took their leave of the attractive appurtenances of the railway, of its technical playthings, its green signals and red flags, the shrill bells of glass and the hard bells of iron, the indefatigable ticking of the telegraph and the yearning swerving gleam of the rails, of the panting breath of the locomotive and the hoarse screech it sent up to the sky, the guard's hail and the wave of the station officials, a wall and a garden fence, of the meagre refreshment room at this forlorn station and the girl who stood behind the bottles and tended a samovar. Especially this girl. Friedrich contemplated her as if she were the last European woman he would be allowed to look at and had to memorize carefully. He recalled Hilde as he might a girl he had talked to twenty years ago. At times he could no longer picture her face. It seemed to him that she had become old and grey in the interim, a grandmother.

They climbed into waggons, halted every twenty-five kilometres, changed horses. Only the driver remained the same throughout the journey. A large part of the convoy had remained behind and was indeed due to be delivered to one of the large collective prisons. Now they consisted only of a few groups. Friedrich and Berzejev, Freyburg and Lion sat in one waggon. Without everyone seeing, Friedrich pressed Berzejev's hand. They sealed a silent compact.

When any of the prisoners removed his cap, one saw the left half of his skull shaved bare, and his face took on the foolish imprint of a lunatic. Each shrank from the other, but each hid his horror under a smile. Only Berzejev had succeeded in bribing the barber. He had his whole scalp shaved bare.

The prisoners sang one song after another. The soldiers and the driver joined in. At times one man would sing alone, and then it was as if he sang with the strength of all. His voice was drowned in the many-voiced refrain, which was like an echo from heaven to earth.

The best singer was Konov, a weaver from Moscow, at whose house a secret printing-press had been discovered. He was on his way to fifteen years' imprisonment.

3

One morning they began their march. Across a desolate flat landscape deployed the trail of human beings with bundles, fetters, sticks in hands.

Of the fifty men thus making their way, in groups of eight, six and ten guarded by sharp bayonets on long rifles, only the oldest manifested fatigue. According to regulations, each was allowed to carry only fifteen poods of baggage. Some who had refused to cut down on their belongings at the last station now discarded useful with unnecessary objects. The soldiers collected all of these and left them behind in the *jurts* which they passed, and which they would revisit on the return journey. Only Berzejev threw nothing away. His bulky pack was carried by the soldiers. He would say a good word to them, stick a cigarette in their mouths, and click his tongue at them as if they were horses.

After they had been marching in silence for a long time, Berzejev ordered: 'Sing'. They sang. But they stopped right after the first verse. A hesitant pause ensued, then the refrain was taken up by a timorous voice, and it was a long time before the others joined in. The melody did not quicken their lagging feet. Exile itself advanced towards them. The railway, horses, carriages and men, all had been left far behind. The sky arched over the flat earth like a round roof of grey lead, soldered around its edges. They were sealed down under the sky. In prison, at least, one knew that a sky still arched above the walls. But here the very freedom was an imprisonment. In the leaden sky there were no bars through which one could spy another sky of blue air. The vastness of this space was more confining than a cell.

Gradually they broke up into ever smaller groups. With tears in their eyes and their beards they bade each other farewell. Friedrich, Berzejev and Lion stayed together. On the first day they still spoke of one or other with whom they had sung together. As soon as they struck up in a threesome the songs that had flowed from everyone's throats a few days previously, they remembered those others whose voices they would never hear again. The songs had become a kind of resonant bond of amity. They had brought strangers together with the power of blood shed in common and pain suffered in common. Then the departed were gradually forgotten. Only now and again did there revive in memory a face that no longer bore a name, a tear in a black beard that no longer belonged to any face, and a word would ring out whose speaker was no longer known.

They were led far and stragglingly, they saw the unpeopled shores of the Obi. The two small settlements of Hurgut and Narym seemed to them large and lively towns. They stayed overnight in Narym. They learned to collect bugs in their fists and drown them in large buckets, also to coax the small white files of lice from the walls into paper cornets and burn them. They began to esteem the lonely scattered jails where they chanced to halt as welcoming homes. They saw distant forest fires, bartered with Chinese merchants from Chifu for Siberian fur gloves and boots of reindeer hide. They listened to the legends of the Yakuts about the Indiguirka River, and the Dogdo rivulet which carries gold along its bed.

Winter came. They became accustomed to 67 degrees Celsius below zero and to the frosted windowpanes of ice in the *jurts*. And they awaited the forty sunless days in the town of Vierchoiansk, the town with the twenty-three houses.

It was laid down that their fixed location should be ten versts from a town, ten versts from a river and ten versts from a high-road. Yet they managed to settle by a river, the Kolyma River. It is bigger than the Rhine, only three towns are situated on it. One had nine inhabitants, another a hundred inhabitants in thirty military barracks. Friedrich, Berzejev and Lion decided on the third town of Sredni Kolymsk. Here there were huts placed far apart and only three houses with glazed windows. But within a circle of many miles it was the only place with a church, a steeple and bells – bells that had been cast in the civilized world and whose ringing was like a mother tongue.

4

The Siberian officials of the Tsar did not always deserve the bad reputation they enjoyed among the inhabitants, the condemned and even their superior authorities. Some, who considered themselves as exiles, and not without reason, were resolved to share the lot of the prisoners rather than intensify it. Many started off by avenging their fate on the condemned but mellowed after a few years when they saw that their harshness brought them no advantage. Arrogance, vanity and terror dwindled, since the controlling authorities were so far away. Others again allowed themselves to be bribed and lived on with a bad conscience. A bad conscience can make both autocrats and thugs indulgent.

Berzejev had made friends with Colonel Lelewicz, a Pole, who had assumed command of an infantry detachment in Siberia in order to have an opportunity of helping his exiled fellow-countrymen. He enjoyed such good connections in Petersburg that he did not need to conceal his sentiments behind a martial loyalty to the Tsar like other officers and officials. With his help Friedrich, Berzejev and Lion established themselves in one of the three houses furnished with windowpanes. Thus they lived in a steady private relationship with the authorities and were allowed to play cards with the officials and conduct political discussions.

Once a week the newspapers arrived, ten days old. The news they spread in this desolation resembled the stars we still see shining in the heavens though they were extinguished centuries ago. Lion affirmed that it was unimportant when one read the papers. For the very transmission of an event changes it and even denies it. That is why we find every report in the newspapers so improbable.

Lion asserted that he had been exiled only on account of his kinship with a well-known revolutionary of the same name, and that he would probably soon be released.

79

He was, in fact, only a mild opponent of the State, favoured the introduction of a constitutional monarchy, modernization of the bureaucracy on the western model and a settlement of domestic political questions on properly applied economic principles. Between two fingers he held his pince-nez which were knotted to a broad black ribbon, threatened with them, designed interweaving arabesques in the air with them, and only settled them on the lower part of his nose when he was compelled to listen, as if Lion wanted to study his opponent better through the glass while nevertheless peering at him only over the rims of the lenses. Everything to do with natural processes was strange and disconcerting to him. He had the same respect for dogs as for wolves and bears. He hardly noticed the passage of the seasons and it made no difference to him whether the temperature was 20 or 60 degrees.

He was a constant herald of the war. 'The Social Democrats in Germany,' he exclaimed, 'have at last revealed their loyalty to the Kaiser. Herr Stücklen says : "We Social Democrats love the country in which we were born, we are better patriots than people think." Noske : "We have never entertained the idea that the frontiers of the Reich can be left unfortified without a considerable defensive army." Because the Social Democrats are for the capital levy on principle, they vote for military credits. Thus they vote for the option of throwing half a million men against the French frontier in four days. The representatives of the International concede one and half milliards to the War Minister. That is war, gentlemen,' concluded Lion, swinging his pince-nez in the air like a flag.

Berzejev and the official Efrejnov were for Germany, suspicious of France. Berzejev defended the German workers. Finally, he even compared the Tsar to the German Kaiser. 'After all,' he said, 'the Kaiser doesn't send anyone to Siberia.'

Efrejnov, who attributed everything bad in Russia to western influences, to which society, the intelligentsia and the Tsar himself were subject, felt offended. His fair beard, his broad shoulders shivered. 'It just shows,' he cried, 'how all alike you are. You believe that somewhere Russia is like the rest of the world, in one small detail at least. Not true. Russia is oriental and everything else is the rotten decaying West. Whether it's your German Kaiser, Berzejev, or your German workers, it's all one. A Kaiser who rules through Parliament and democracy, that's already the beginning of Socialism. The Kaiser, the republic, Marxism, all western ideas. The Tsar in Russia is more democratic than a socialist parliamentarian. He is sovereign by the will of the people and of the land it cultivates. The Tsar is the product of the Russian peasant. He looks after the affairs of state for which the people have no time. When did your dissatisfaction begin? Since you looked to the West and envied its civilization. Witte goes to do business with the American Jews. The Anglomaniac snob Isvolski is sent out into the world so that he can report what ties they are wearing in London and Paris. And thus you destroy the old holy autocracy of the Tsars.'

For some time Lion had been drawing restless curves in the air with his pince-nez. 'Do you imagine,' he shouted, 'that we can shut ourselves off from the West? We can't compete with world economy.

'Russia is not going to remain a nation of peasants. It is becoming industrialized. But industry dictates the political set-up. Two-thirds of our industries are in foreign hands. We produce our iron and petroleum so slowly that they do not suffice even for our own feeble production. Our coal-mines deliver only 2,250 million poods as against 18 milliards in Germany and 32 milliards in the United States. The average income of a Russian subject amounts to 53 roubles a year, of a Frenchman 233, an Englishman 273, an American 345. The average Russian saves only 16 roubles a year. Our national debt amounts to 9 milliards, that is 2 roubles 80 kopecks a head. But England, which in your view belongs to the degenerate West, has a national budget of 160 million pounds sterling and underpins its economy with a further 170 millions.'

Nothing availed against Lion's figures, which he recited without the least hesitation, like a poem. As he uttered them, he drew them briskly in the air as if writing them with chalk on a blackboard. Efrejnov shook his head. Evidently he considered statistics, like Marxism, to be a product of the West and figures as crimes like assassinations. Lion had probably been sent to Siberia with more justification than the others. He regarded the ikon in the corner and the small red lamp lit a soothing gentle consolation in his heart.

5

Friedrich lit the slender candle of transparent paraffin wax.

From the ground the earth's frozen breath entered the room like a steeply rising wind. Around the house sang the still, aching cold. It was like the singing of telegraph wires.

Friedrich imagined to himself that there, in front of the house, in the impenetrable darkness, stood the smooth-planed tall posts topped with their flowers of white porcelain, linked by wires with the living world, whose forlorn voice they transformed into the clear, comforting and trustful monotony of a lullaby. When he lay down to sleep there flashed through his first slumber a rapid fancy, less than a thought and more than a dream, that his sleep would carry him towards a morning in the middle of the lively and bustling city. Berzejev still spoke to him for long stretches and did not wait for a reply. He loved his quiet younger comrade, his thin face and reserved look, and the courage with which he had joined the Revolution. 'He has no discretion,' observed Berzejev. 'His rashness hinders him from anticipating situations. But when they come he bears them steadfastly. He is easily inspired and easily dis-illusioned. But despondency and enthusiasm are only phy-siological phenomena. In reality he is melancholy, uniformly melancholy.' And Berzejev said out loud :

'This poor Efrejnov is confused by Lion. He is too unsuspecting to find arguments. I could have found them for him. Russia's faults are really the consequence of hasty endeavours to copy the West. In all probability, Russia would be sound and rich without the stupid aspiration held by a certain section of its ruling class to become civilized, and to be regarded in the fashionable spas of Western Europe as proper Europeans. The bigoted Agrarians are no less right than we ourselves, the thoroughgoing revolu-tionaries. They lack only understanding. Everything that lies in the middle, between thoroughgoing reaction and thoroughgoing revolution, is foolish in Russia. The bour-geois class has developed before there was a place ready for it. Now it is demanding its industries. The Tsar is helpless.

83

He is turning himself into an Emperor on the old Western model, rather like the present German Kaiser. Autocracy gives way to bureaucracy and the officials are the vanguard of the bourgeoisie. It begins with the entry of the sons of the nobility and the rich bourgeoisie into official posts, that is, into the great cities. And the cities are the enemy of the countryside. The intelligentsia follows. It is the outpost of the Revolution. The semi-revolutionary ideals of the intelligentsia are foreign to the instincts of the Russian people. The cruelty of the Agrarian autocracy is really closer to them. You see, therefore, the imminence of an explosion. The intellectual bureaucrat renders the Agrarians impotent. He can topple the Tsar but not govern the people. His dominance will be an insignificant intermission. It is we who hold the power. Russia can only become a proletarian, not a bourgeois, republic. Only a war is needed, and the old Russia is done for. And the war is coming; we shan't be staying in Siberia much longer.'

Flour was unaffordable. In this region the housewives could bake only three times a year. Bread was scarcer than meat. For the first time Friedrich felt the immediate relation between sun and earth. For the first time he understood the simple meaning of the prayer man addresses to Heaven for his daily bread. At the breadless table where he sat down twice a day he thought of the bakers' shops in the bustling towns. He closed his eyes. He conjured up the different colours of the flour and the different shapes of the loaves.

'What are you dreaming about?' asked Berzejev.

'Of bread. When I picture the world from which we are exiled, I think of quite trivial things – flat matches, for instance, for the waistcoat pocket and round lids for beer-mugs, inkwells one can open by pressing, celluloid paper-knives and quite ordinary things like a picture-postcard. I remember one that used to hang in the shop-window of the stationer's on the corner of the street where I lived. It was old and yellowed, had been in the window for years. It was a miserable little stationer's and an ugly card. It had a wide gold edge, speckled black by flies. It showed a well-known picture. On the globe, poised in space – the space, if I remember rightly, was pale blue – sits a woman with a blindfold on the North Pole.'

'Yes, yes,' said Berzejev, 'I've seen that picture too. Wait a minute, I think the woman held something in her hand and she wore a watery blue dress. But I don't recall the wide gold margin.'

'But it was a wide gold margin,' insisted Friedrich, 'and fly-speckled, and there was a yellow post-box at the street-corner. You could stick down a letter and push it inside and even hear the way it fell – with a thud if the box was empty and with a rustle if there were letters already inside.'

'Let's stick to bread,' said Berzejev. 'You're distracting me from it. To begin with, there were two main kinds, white and black. Once in France – I was there with my father when I was fourteen – I ate hard, white, long batons of bread with a golden-brown crust. But the Russian country bread, black and reddish, with rather coarse soft grains, is the one I like best.'

'I remember,' continued Friedrich, 'how it smelled when one passed a baker's shop.'

'Especially at night!' cried Berzejev.

'Yes, at night, when it was winter, you were struck all of a sudden by a warmth from the cellars, almost like an animal warmth.'

'A bread-like warmth,' exulted Berzejev.

85

'And in the morning, in summer, when I woke very early and went into the street, the white baker's boys were trotting around with covered baskets. How those baskets smelled! And you could hear the birds singing then, because the streets were still quiet.'

They fell silent for a time.

Suddenly Berzejev said: 'How stupid we have become!'

'No, not stupid,' cried Friedrich, 'only human. We were ideologists, not human beings. We wanted to reshape the world and we are dependent on postcards and must eat bread.'

'It's because not everyone has bread,' said Berzejev quietly, 'that we are sitting here. How simple it all is. One doesn't need theory or economics. Because not everyone has bread – very simple and quite stupid.'

'R. might have put that better,' thought Friedrich. 'R. might possibly have said: "We want to help. But we are not born for that. Because of our impotence, nature has endowed us with too strong a love, it exceeds our powers. We are like a man who is unable to swim, but who jumps in after a drowning man and goes under himself. But we have to jump. Sometimes we help the other, but usually both of us go under. And no one knows whether, at the last moment, one feels happiness or a kind of bitter anger." '

'When I was fourteen years old,' began Berzejev, 'my father took me on a journey. I saw foreign railway stations for the first time, and that was really the best part. Do you still remember railway stations?'

They both thought of the station they had last seen.

'Did you see that girl?' asked Friedrich.

And Berzejev knew at once which girl he meant.

'Yes,' he said, 'she was standing behind the buffet and gave me a glass of tea. She had her plaits braided in two round coils over her ears.'

'And red cheeks.'

They spoke of the strange girl as of a lost loved one.

'But there was something else besides railway stations when I was fourteen,' resumed Berzejev, 'and that was that there was a woman in our compartment with whom my father got into conversation. He treated her to chocolate bonbons, lifted her heavy cases down from the luggage-rack and put them back again, took the lady to the dining-car and said to the waiter : "A table for three, the fourth seat's empty, understood?" "Yes, your Honour," said the waiter. For my father was a high official, a landowner and a gentleman. You could see that at once. I spent much of the time in the corridor, which I enjoyed. You really feel that you are travelling there. When you stand the train goes faster, and then you fancy yourself freer and closer to the attendant. When a station arrives you climb out quickly. And even the lavatory is fine. I often used to go in there and if anyone rattled the door vigorously I stayed in all the longer. Once, when I went back to the compartment, the lady gave a start, screamed out, and my father was looking through the window at the landscape. I sat down in my corner, covered myself with my overcoat and pretended to be asleep. Then my father went out, I noticed how he stepped over my legs. The next moment the lady pulled the coat off my face and kissed me quickly on the mouth and sat down again. So I thought: "She kisses me so that I shouldn't be naughty or tell tales at home." But we met her again at Nice. She had arranged it with my father, and once, in the afternoon, she took me into her room. We were staying at the same hotel. It was already evening and the dinner-gong was sounding when I came out of her room. My father was waiting for me in the corridor. I tried to run past him, he grabbed me and gave me a box on the ear.'

'And then?'

'Just think, after that I never spoke another word to my father until his death, which I only heard of two days later, not a word! I began to hate him. I saw his fleshy mouth under the worthy mottled moustache. As soon as we got back he sent me to the military academy. He wrote to me twice a year and I wrote to him. They were like the letters of a professional letter-writer. But when I went home, for Easter, we kissed and did not speak and the whole year I used to dread the kiss that awaited me.'

'He should have spoken,' said Friedrich.

'Then I would probably not be here,' said Berzejev.

6

Sometimes Colonel Lelewicz came himself. Sometimes he would send one of his friends. He brought bread, tinned food, newspapers. At irregular intervals there was a visit from Len-Min-Tsin, the Chinese trader, with newspapers, books and cheap pornography. This consisted of packets of postcards like those offered to foreigners in the dazzling nights of great cities by timid little dealers with encouraging whispers. The Chinaman purveyed the postcards in series through the lost townships of Siberia and lent them out like books. He would then collect them again from his subscribers and exchange them for new ones. The pictures were worn like old playing-cards by the covetous fingers of many hundreds. Efrejnov, Lion and Berzejev scrutinized the cards together in unpolitical and purely sexual accord. Efrejnov kept a dignified silence as he became engrossed in the details. He puckered his eyebrows, combed his fair beard with his fingers, narrowed his eyelids and peered at the cards through a narrow slit with the appraising glance of a connoisseur. Against his will, he simultaneously opened his bewhiskered lips in the same measure as he closed his eyelids. His tongue crept inquisitively between his teeth, he began to smile, his face relaxed and, despite the powerful neck on which it rested, despite the beard in which it was framed and embedded, acquired a boyish expression. Lion held his pince-nez in his hand, hard against his eyes, and tapped one foot incessantly, causing his body to break into a delicate rocking tremor. Berzejev was red under the normal brown of his countenance and it seemed, not that his skin was flushed, but that the red complexion of his second inner self was appearing through the brown of the outer man. Impatient as he was, he wanted to turn over faster than the others, who appeared to have a more thorough approach.

'That's my friend,' thought Friedrich. 'He's loyal, he has a fine passion, he is kind, clever and cautious. One can rely on him. He can command a regiment. He can stand up to hunger, but a postcard. . . . If I take the pictures away from him now. . . .' He stepped to the table and took the pack that lay in front of Berzejev. Berzejev raised his hand to rescue his cards from Friedrich's grasp. But he did not lower it, he held it in the air for a while as if taking an oath. Suddenly he laughed out loud.

'I felt sorry for you,' said Friedrich.

'Perhaps it was ridiculous,' said Berzejev. They said no more about it.

But a few days later Berzejev suddenly brought out : 'I have slept with Efrejnov's wife. He was with Lion in our room.'

And, as Friedrich did not enquire further, very quickly and seriously : 'I only wanted to let you know.'

That was all. But as if Berzejev's adventure had opened some new door in his memory Friedrich began to think of the millions of far-off women with the yearning with which he had thought of the taste, the smell, the shape of bread. He recalled a hundred little events without significance and without a sequel. The platform of a street-car, in front of him a woman, arm elevated, hand on one of the leather straps dangling from the carriage roof. Distinct, the line of her taut breast, her neck. He can no longer see her face. He hears the gentle tripping of a young girl through a narrow quiet street, the echo that meets her shoes like an affectionate answer from the cobbles. Hilde's dove-grey narrow shoe on the red velvet of the carriage. Grey on red. They were the colours of his love. He thought of them as a patriot thinks of his country's flag. The little glove shop, the patient expectation of the outspread fingers and the delicate play of the hands. The narrow bracelet between the sleeve and the edge of the glove. The warmth his hand encountered when he stroked her arm. Many fleeting contacts, intentionally willed, intentionally feigned, scarce-born anticipations of a contact, others that flitted like shadows over the bodies. He tears up the letter. She cries. He does not recall distinctly seeing her tears. He believes he only heard them. Hilde goes through the door of the little café, behind the half-curtained window pane her outline shows for a moment longer in the street. She disappears in the city. He steps outside, she is no longer there. Why has he been in any doubt that he loves her? He had been ashamed before his conscience, before R., before his ambition.

For weeks now he has spoken only when it was absolutely essential. He has heard the endless discussions as a confused and meaningless din. Proletariat, autocracy, finance, ruling class, militarism. Simple formulae, one had to make use of them in order to act. But they embraced only a minor part of what they aspired to contain. Life is stuck fast in these concepts like a fully-grown child in too-short clothes. A single hour of life comprises a thousand enigmatic stirrings of the nerves, the muscles, the brain and a single large empty word wants to express them all.

There was at this time only one word that had any meaning: Flight!

One could flee. He felt as if he had been abstracted from his own life for years and as if he were living somebody else's. Somewhere his own waited like a good home, unjustly abandoned. To flee, to escape the leaden sky, the breadless table. As yet the idea hung only in the air, like a child's red balloon. Life was short. Sixty years of freedom were less than ten years of Siberia.

'What's up with you?' asked Berzejev.

The days were still long. But clouds came in the early evening, the moon destroyed them. They were there again in the morning cradling the red sun. It was an effort for it to rise. They prepared themselves for winter. The Cheldony said it would come earlier than usual, that winter was already upon them. The Chinaman would fail to appear, the newspapers become fewer, one must stock up with candles and oil.

'I must escape,' said Friedrich.

'Out of the question now, we're going to be free.'

'Depend on me, I think of it every day.'

At that moment Lion burst through the door. He waved a newspaper.

The heir to the Austrian throne had been shot.

7

That night they slept peacefully, as if it were quite an ordinary night.

Meanwhile war was brewing in Europe. In the barracks trumpets sounded the alarm. Large posters were put up at all the street-corners of towns small and great. The trains rolled from the stations garlanded with green and the men had military uniforms and caps and rifles. All the women wept.

One day Colonel Lelewicz appeared in Kolymsk with a few friends. There was nothing striking about that. Small squads had already passed through. Efrejnov rejoiced. The newspapers arrived more quickly, as if impelled by the speed of the reports they contained. The whole region was almost invigorated.

Lelewicz bade farewell to his friend.

He left a blue packet lying on Berzejev's table. Berzejev did not notice it. He was standing at the door. He accompanied the colonel. Lelewicz climbed into the saddle. He waved for the last time. Berzejev turned back into the room. He sighted the packet, quickly seized it and ran outside after the colonel. He shouted, Lelewicz seemed not to hear. He was only a small blue-black speck on the horizon.

Friedrich held Berzejev fast. 'That's for us!' he said with eyes staring, pale, breathless and unable to speak.

When Efrejnov awoke next morning, Friedrich and Berzejev had disappeared.

8

They were afraid of attracting the attention of the secret police more readily if they stayed together. So they decided to separate for a few days, then to meet up again, and to make the journey to the first large town in stages. The first to arrive was to wait for the other, the latecomer to move on later. If one of them were captured, the other would realize that he must not show himself for the time being. They were ready at any moment to fall into the hands of the police. But each of the pair trembled more for the other than for himself. The constant apprehension sealed their friendship more than the need to face every danger together would have done, and bestowed on them in turn all the kinds and grades of love included in the terms of friendship : they were fathers, brothers and children to one another. Always, when they came together again after several days, they fell into each other's arms, kissed and laughed. Even when neither had encountered any real danger on the way, each yet remained shaken by the dangers he had imagined as threatening the other. And although their splitting up had the object of saving at least one of them from arrest, both had nevertheless privately decided to give themselves up if anything should befall the other.

At last they reached European Russia. They saw the country's warlike enthusiasm. These were the last happier moments of the Tsar, as it later appeared, almost – as it were – brought about by a conscious intent of world history to mislead a doomed system. The Radicals embraced the Conservatives and, as always when strangers come together in danger and opponents are reconciled, there was faith in a miraculous rebirth of the country because the miracle of fraternization is enough to make men believe in one even more improbable. Enmity is familiar to human nature, while reconciliation is foreign to it. Patriotic alliances were hurriedly formed. A hundred new names and insignia were invented. People marched through the streets and smashed German shop-signs.

'How puzzling,' said Friedrich to Berzejev, as they sat in their hotel room, 'that the individuals of which the mass is composed surrender their characteristics, lose even their primary instincts. The individual loves his life and fears death. Together with others, he discards life and despises death. The individual does not want to join the army and pay taxes. With others, he voluntarily enlists and empties his pockets. And the one is as genuine as the other.'

'I shall be interested to see,' said Berzejev, 'how long this enthusiasm will last, and whether one cannot turn it into its opposite. I shall also be interested to see whether things are exactly like this, or much the same, in other countries. Lion was right. The German Social Democrats are marching.'

According to documents that Lelewicz had procured for them, they were due to enlist for a year's service in an artillery regiment in Volynia. They had the following expedients: either they enlisted and awaited an opportunity to be captured and then to escape from captivity again; or they hid in the country for the time being and waited for an opportunity to reach a foreign country with the aid of their friends, there to be interned as civilians. At that time they did not contemplate a third possibility. Chance helped them.

This was that, in Kharkov, they heard from a hotel porter due to enlist in the same regiment, that it was already in occupied territory, on Austrian soil. They could therefore depart, fail to report, but mingle with the inhabitants of one of the occupied towns and, with the aid of Friedrich's old connections at the frontier, play the part of honest citizens under the occupation.

9

Thus he found himself once more at 'The Ball and Chain'. Yet again it stood in his path. He left Berzejev to wait in the large empty tap-room and climbed the stairs that led to old Parthagener's room.

Friedrich looked through the keyhole; the door was locked. Old Parthagener was sleeping on the green sofa, as always in the afternoon from two to four. He slept as if to refute the war. The old furniture was still in the room. An unfolded newspaper lay on the table, watched by the blue spectacles. Friedrich wondered whether to wake the old man. It seemed dangerous to wait. At any moment a patrol might enter the tavern. He knocked. The old man jumped up. 'Who's there?' Still the same cry. He opened the door. 'Ah, it's you! We've been expecting you for a long time. Kapturak heard a week ago that you'd escaped with your comrade Berzejev. You've been gone a long time, poor young man! You must have been through a lot! But now you're here! Was it really necessary?'

'So nothing has changed!' thought Friedrich. 'Kapturak and Parthagener have been expecting me as if I had gone across to fetch a "batch".' And to Parthagener: 'So Kapturak is here?'

'And why not! He has enlisted as a medical orderly. Didn't you see the big Red Cross flag on our roof? We are, you might say, a hospital without patients. Kapturak marched in with the victorious army in the very first week. Just a common medical orderly! But actually involved in espionage. With connections with the army command. He brings us healthy soldiers and we treat them with various prescriptions. We give them civilian clothing and documents, injections, narcotics, symptoms of paralysis and defective vision. Unfortunately, I am quite alone. My sons have enlisted. At this very time. Not that I fear for their lives! A Parthagener doesn't get killed in the war! But I'm an old man and can't cope with the many deserters.'

More and more deserters came to Parthagener. The fear of a war that was only a possibility had turned into the much greater fear of a war that already existed. The old man sat in his inn and sold remedies against danger as an apothecary might sell powders against fever.

'And where is your friend?' asked the old man. 'He's waiting downstairs!'

Parthagener put on his glasses and combed his fine white beard before the mirror. Then he turned round again. Until now he had spoken personally. Henceforth he was the official landlord, ready to offer a stranger what he had – quiet dignity and spiritual comfort.

In the early evening twilight, Kapturak arrived. He was in uniform and seemed more composed than in more settled times. Then he had been an adventurer. Now, in the midst of the great adventure, he was an honest man who had not abandoned his civilian calling.

It was quiet in the tap-room. At times the heavy step of a patrol could be heard, making its way through the town. It was possible to forget that here the war, which had been in preparation so long, was at home, here on this frontier which was its homeland. Old Parthagener sat over a large book and calculated. Berzejev slept, head on the table-top. Only his tangled brown hair was visible.

'Are you going to stay with him?' asked Kapturak. The glance he cast in Berzejev's direction was physical, like an outstretched index finger.

'He intends to go to Switzerland via Rumania, the Balkans, Italy. I would rather go by Vienna.'

'You both leave tomorrow!' decided Kapturak. 'As Swiss Red Cross. I'll arrange the departure.'

They slept in the bar-parlour. Friedrich was woken a few times by distant shots which rang with a long echo through the still night, and by the distant pale gleam of the searchlights which lit up the horizon and the windows for short seconds. He saw himself, in a dream, running along a narrow path between fields. The path led into a wood. It was night. A broad band of light from a searchlight sped over the fields to find the track along which Friedrich was running. The track had no end. The dark mass of the wood was visible close by. But the path took unexpected bends, evaded a rock and a puddle, and whenever Friedrich decided to abandon it and run straight across the fields the wood disappeared from his sight. A naked sky, shamelessly stripped by white searchlights, lay flat and endless over the world. Hastily he sought again for the treacherous path and he ran, carefully despite his haste, one foot in front of the other, so as not to step to one side and lose sight of the wood.

In the morning he walked once more through the little town. The shops were closed. No one showed himself at the windows of the low houses. Soldiers were encamped on the square market-place. The horses whinnied. Enormous cauldrons gave forth greasy warm odours. The supply waggons rolled incessantly and apparently aimlessly over the uneven cobblestones. On the stone threshold of a house whose door was closed sat a soldier. He held a sack between his knees, bent his head over it and looked inside. As Friedrich passed he closed the sack with startled haste and lifted his head. He had a pale broad face with faded brows over narrow light-grey eyes. His cap sat crooked on his hair and squashed one ear. His yellow uniform of coarse linen was too small and his broad shoulders bulged out the upper part of the sleeves. He was like a lunatic in a strait-jacket. A gradual fear spread over his face. His much too short lips, which could never quite be closed, revealed the gums over his long yellow teeth. He gave the appearance of laughing and crying, friendliness and rage. 'I've frightened you!' said Friedrich. The soldier nodded. 'What have you got in the sack? Don't be afraid!' The soldier opened it quickly and let Friedrich look inside. Friedrich saw silver spoons, chains, candlesticks and watches. 'What are you going to do with these?' The soldier shrugged his shoulders and held his head on one side like a naughty child. At last he begged: 'Give me your watch!' 'You've got so many!' said Friedrich, 'I've none.' 'Let's see!' pleaded the soldier. He stood up and put his hands in Friedrich's pockets. He found papers, pencils, an old newspaper, a knife, a handkerchief. 'No, you haven't got one!' said the soldier. 'Here, help yourself!' And he opened the sack. 'I don't want a watch!' said Friedrich. 'Go on. You must take one!' insisted the man and put a watch in his coat pocket.

Friedrich went away. The soldier ran after him, the sack swinging in his hand. 'Halt!' he cried. And, as Friedrich stood still: 'Give me back the watch!' He took it back again with a trembling hand. Officers returned from breakfast, with jingling spurs, belted waists, with the warlike elegance that confers the badge of manhood on them together with a certain resemblance to female models. They swayed their hips, at which pistols hung like pieces of jewellery in their cases. The soldiers in the streets saluted. And the officers responded gaily and lightly. As they passed among respectful salutes, dumb submissiveness, infatuated devotion, they resembled society ladies passing through a ballroom.

Ambulances arrived from which wounded men with white bandages were removed like plaster figures from a drawer; a horse lay dying in the middle of the street, without anyone taking any notice; an officer rode by. He came up to the level of the house-tops and seemed to be visiting the world like a blue deity.

They left the same day for Rumania. Berzejev went on to Switzerland via Greece and Italy, Friedrich continued to Vienna by way of Hungary. They arranged to meet in Zürich. They travelled with Red Cross armbands and with identification papers of Kapturak's manufacture as members of a Swiss medical mission.

10

In Rumania Friedrich parted from his friend. At the time, when I heard that he was going to Vienna, I found it inexplicable that he did not make the detour by way of Italy and Switzerland together with Berzejev. And when, in the field, I received the first letter from Friedrich for a long time – I quote a typical passage in one of the following pages – I still assumed that it was something important, probably on behalf of his Party, that took him to Austria. But he had nothing to do there. I cannot conceive that a man who had lived for over a year in a Siberian prison camp should return to a city in order to meet an acquaintance, or even a woman. Yet Friedrich seems to have had no other reason. Savelli was no longer in Vienna. The Ukrainian comrade P. had been living for a year in a concentration camp for civilian internees in Austria. R. had moved to Switzerland – a month before the outbreak of war. Friedrich could not even go safely through the streets without military papers. People – as one knows – had all become the shadows of their documents. Friedrich's age group had long ago been called up. He must have appeared suspicious to every policeman on the streets. The large mobilization notices, in which he was named, clung faded and tattered to the walls, as if in confirmation that the members of this age-group had already fallen and begun to rot. Friedrich, to whom a definite citizenship could not be allotted, could be arrested and end up in a camp. At the frontier and en route he had stated that he had come from Rumania to enlist. People had believed him, there were many like him on the train. A gendarme who checked his papers told him as much. Men came from distant countries to take up a rifle. Here, too, the trains were decorated with foliage. The soldiers sang different songs and wore different colours from those in Russia. A month before they had all been in mufti, both here and over there, barely distinguishable. Why, then should they all at once be able to sing? They had never sung before when they had sat in trains as travellers in perfumery, as lawyers, as officials going on leave or returning to their duties. Had they no respect for death? Did they respect it only when it appeared with the festive insignia which they liked to bestow on it at proper times and in proper churchyards, at coffin-makers and in funeral parlours?

'I gradually came to recognize my old anger against authority,' Friedrich wrote to me later in the field. 'I was rebelling against authority as it is at the present time. For it is not based on legal assumptions. The book-keeper who goes off singing to the war is no more a hero than the policeman is a policeman, the minister a minister, or the Kaiser a Kaiser. One does not see this in times of peace. But now the hundred thousand lawyers and headmasters who have suddenly turned into officers, expose this illegality which applies even to the regular officers. There is no doubt that society reveals its identity, however it disguises itself.

'I was in the Union of Young Workers, which you know. The Thursday evening meetings still take place. I read the programme in the entrance-hall. These were the titles of the lectures: "The Central Powers and the War", "Socialism and Germany", "Tsarism and the Proletariat", "The Middle European idea and Freedom of the Peoples". I sought the chairman, a young metal worker. Despite his youth, he was currently exempted from military service because he worked in a munitions factory and on account of his expert knowledge. "Oh, Comrade!" said the young man, overjoyed. He wore a badge in his buttonhole whose design I could not quite make out and which combined a cross, a star and a hammer. A draughtsman in the munitions factory had designed it and it had become officially adopted as the insignia of the heroes of the home front as the metal workers are known. "How marvellous, that you've escaped!" said the young man. "When do you enlist? Will you give us a talk beforehand? There aren't many of us now, most have joined up!" While he was speaking he had the cheerfulness of the president of a festival committee. On his table lay piles of pink field postcards, there was an ashtray he had made himself out of the grenades he helped to produce. On the wall hung one of the familiar prints showing Karl Marx, and a red flag wrapped up with string leaned in a corner. It was rather like a rolled-up sunshade, the ones the flower-sellers spread over their stalls on hot summer days. And because it was snowing outside, it seemed to me in a fit of strange confusion that the flag was really an umbrella.'

He remembered Grünhut as one remembers a medicine one has already used a few times with success. Grünhut was a lost individual, even a war could not relieve him of his excommunication. And as society was waging war, Friedrich concluded with the consistency of a man who has not yet experienced a war, that the previously convicted must be normal.

Grünhut jumped up. 'Come in, come in,' he said, and drew Friedrich to the table and lit the gas-lamp which began to diffuse a humming green chill. However, he endeavoured to warm his frozen hands at the flame.

Friedrich told of his escape. Grünhut walked around in the room and rubbed his hands. 'What heroism!' he said. 'You've earned a decoration even before going into the field! It ought to be published in the papers! What a hero! What a hero!'

And he began to talk of the imminent siege of the city of Paris, of Hindenburg's march towards Petersburg, of a regiment that had passed under his window that very day on its way to the station, and of his hopes of being rehabilitated at last. He now referred to his old unhappy story as 'a tragic case'. He had put in a request to the regiment in which he had served as a one-year volunteer years ago; he had been a sergeant and been considered for a commission. He had kept a copy, which he took from his pocket and began to read aloud. In it he talked about the exceptional times, about the Fatherland and the Kaiser, about his 'youthful misdemeanour' and his yearning to die as a soldier and a gentleman, to make up for a wasted life with a splendid death. Despite his age, he wanted to go to the front.

He wiped the sweat from his forehead although his red hands betrayed that he was freezing. He was hot and cold at the same time. His head was in quite another climate than his body. At the moment, so Grünhut said, there were no addresses to write. A large tailoring firm, which had a contract for uniforms, gave him so-called home work. He fetched twenty pairs of military trousers and a hundred and fifty buttons from the workshop every third day and delivered the trousers with the buttons sewn on three days later. He delivered only good work. Others were satisfied with drawing one thread through each hole in the button. Then, the first time a soldier fastened his braces, the button tore off. People had no conscience. But Grünhut sewed the buttons on so carefully that they were as firm as iron. Although spot-checks were made on all the other home workers, he was taken on trust. Also he received a higher wage. Only now things weren't too good. Frau Tarka was gradually losing her clientèle. The men were enlisting, the women becoming nurses. They gradually learned to be careful and to avoid becoming pregnant. It was practice. Sexual matters could no longer remain secret. And the girls' fear of their fathers also grew less with the times. So Frau Tarka pestered him. She demanded more money for his room. Letting to refugees from the east was so profitable now. He put her off with his prospects of rehabilitation.

'Shall we go and eat?'

Yes, they went to the canteen.

The weather had suddenly changed, a warm wind blew and turned the snow into rain. The slightly wounded and convalescents walked with sticks, with black and white bandages, many on the arms of dark-blue nurses. The street-lamps had been turned down, the lights in the shop-windows were put out early, many shops had closed because their proprietors had been called up. The lowered iron doors were reminiscent of graves, and the bills that gave the reason for the absence of the shopkeepers were like the inscriptions on tombstones. In many streets it was so dark that the stars were visible between the ragged clouds. It was an invasion of nature among the houses and street-lamps. The rows of windows were blind. Sky and clouds were mirrored in the windowpanes.

The feebly lit room of the canteen seemed brighter and friendlier than in peacetime. More women than men now sat at the long tables. They talked of sons and husbands, took crumpled field postcards and old newspapers from hidden pockets. A few grey-haired men, who greeted Grünhut with a brief silence, spoke of politics. Grünhut, whom the old men called Doctor, explained to them the strategic position of the Allied armies and comforted them over the advance of the Russians into Galicia with an allusion to Napoleon, who in 1812 had to thank his very advance for his misfortunes. 'I reported to the military authorities yesterday of my own free will!' he said, as a final and conclusive proof that the victory of the Central Powers was certain. The old men shook their heads. 'How old are you?' they asked. 'Fifty-two!' said Grünhut, with the same emphasis with which he had previously said 'thirty thousand prisoners.'

Friedrich suddenly noticed, hanging on the walls, a large coloured oleograph of the Kaiser in coronation robes. The portrait had already been there in peacetime, but so high up on the wall and so dusty that it had always been taken for a landscape. Now it hung in a more prominent position, like a renewed plighting of troths by the beggars and the poor who came there.

11

Friedrich still had enough money to last him for about a month. Berzejev had divided the ready money with him. Friedrich was waiting for a letter from his friend in Zürich. He had no proof of identity to satisfy the police about himself. He lived in his old room at the tailor's, who had been rejected for the time being on grounds of general physical debility. This good fortune made him affable. He warned Friedrich against his wife and advised him to tell her that he was expecting a telegram to report for duty any day.

Friedrich was afraid of the neighbours, an anonymous denunciation, a policeman's glance, and even Grünhut the patriot.

He wanted to see Hilde again. He wrote to her, asking her to come to the café. He waited in the corner; an old gentleman sat opposite him, a newspaper in front of his face. Only his snow-white hair was visible, parted in the middle. He did not stir. He did not lay the newspaper down, nor did he turn it over. It was as if he had fallen asleep but went on reading through closed eyelids. A full glass of water which he had not touched stood on his table, covered by a page of the newspaper. He was probably holding quite an old issue of the paper, one announcing the outbreak of war. He could no longer put it down. On the wall to the right hung a long narrow mirror which had never been completely visible because it had always been obscured by a customer's back. It only provided a fleeting glimpse to the passer-by. Now, for the first time, Friedrich could see his face even though he was sitting down. Only two lamps burnt in the whole room. The wall where the mirror was still lay in the darkening grey of the departing day, and the mirror seemed far removed from the lighted part of the room. It held the image of one of the burning lamps, diminished in its unfathomable depths. Friedrich beheld his face like that of a stranger. If he turned his glance sideways without moving his head he could see his profile, and it alarmed him that he could scarcely recognize himself. His mouth was narrow, his lower lip projected and pulled the chin up with it. His hair was receding, his forehead bulged white and gleaming, and the first hint of a silvery sheen showed at his temples. His nose drooped gently and wearily over his mouth.

Night already lay behind the windows when Hilde entered. He went towards her. He looked in her face for a long time, as he had just been looking in the mirror. He wanted to find changes in her, too, shadows cast by the times. But the months had passed over her smooth dark face like harmless caressing summer airs. Time had found no place on her cheeks to leave a trace behind. The dark gleam of her eyes, the glimmer of the soft silvery down on her skin, the red bow of her lips, the graceful hesitance of her body, which seemed to reflect before every movement as if the limbs had sense and the nerves intelligence – all these were for ever. Friedrich waited for the first sound of her voice as for a gift. He wanted to see and hear all at once. The waiter, hailed by her, came as a deliverance. 'What would you like to order?' he asked. And once again he heard her voice.

She had been informed of his fate. She had often revisited the café. Once R. had sat down at her table and told her about Friedrich. But now it was wartime. And he had a twofold reason for fighting against Tsarism. The cause of freedom was now so splendidly identical with the cause of the Fatherland that all class distinctions and class conflicts were annulled. She was well aware of this. At last she had found an opportunity to get to know the people, for she nursed the wounded in hospital every morning. And finally came the inevitable question : 'When are you joining up?'

'Next week,' he said mechanically.

Could he come round tomorrow afternoon? Some of her old friends would be there, many of course in uniform.

'No!' he said. But he already saw a shadow on her face and was touched by the fact that she was sad and might miss him.

'Yes!' he corrected himself. 'I'll come.'

In the entrance hall at Herr von Maerker's he already noted signs that the Fatherland was in danger. On the clothes-racks at either side of the mirror hung officers' caps and blue cloaks with metal buttons, and two sabres leaned in the stands appointed for umbrellas in times of peace. As Friedrich handed his hat to the servant girl it seemed to him that she hung it on a rather remote hook with faint disdain, alongside two dark forlorn civilian overcoats. The servant girl had a distant resemblance to a camp-follower.

Most of the friends of the household had joined up. Herr von Maerker himself had become a captain and was currently commandant of a railway station. Twice a day he went to the station and observed the departing regiments and the arriving transports of wounded with an enthusiastic interest. The unwonted exercise did him good. Every day, for decades, he had walked along the same two streets. The sojourn at a station that he had only fleetingly traversed twice a year, on his departure for and his return from the holidays, gave him the pleasant illusion after years of monotonous office work of finding himself caught up in an exciting life. He had to thank his connections at the War Ministry for various items of knowledge about goings-on in politics and at G.H.Q., and for the comforting feeling that he would remain at one of the stations in Vienna for as long as it was possible. Naturally, he did not for a moment think that the protection he enjoyed was inconsistent with his love for the Fatherland. He lacked any understanding of the close connection between patriotism and danger to life. He did not take into account that the direct consequence of war was death, rather than variety. After all, like so many of his social class, he hardly realized that the phrase 'Fallen on the Field of Honour' necessarily implied the irrevocable end of the fallen.

Herr von Maerker's housekeeper now went about with the cheering prospect of becoming the bride of her employer after victory. In its very first months the war had upset a few social prejudices which, despite their stupidity, had nevertheless been more moralistic than the war. A new era was seen as imminent. Because it had become necessary to endow proletarians with the aristocratic attributes of heroes and knights, members of the social class to which Herr von Maerker belonged imagined that they had become democratic. Some young women, so-called 'liaisons' of the sons of the aristocracy and high finance, were fortunate enough, through a quick wartime wedding, to become the legitimate spouses of their princes instead, as was usually the case in peacetime, of acquiring a drapery shop or a glove business as a peace-settlement. Through the mediation of their pretty daughters, a few hundred of the lower middle class acquired connections with elevated circles and got into the army medical service when they enlisted. Patriotic unity was therefore no longer a matter for doubt. All the ladies were nurses or manifested some kind of lively charitable impulse. They went so far as to send unknown war widows articles of clothing that would otherwise have been given to the sewing-women in order to forestall any demands for increased wages. Golden wedding-rings were exchanged for iron ones, even though there was some willingness to retain the precious stones. Watch-chains, especially unfashionable ones, were also exchanged. Wherever one looked there was iron. Many sons found themselves risking their lives, to the gratification of their parents. Even the ne'er-do-wells who had squandered money, were forgiven, since they were now heroes and no longer capable of squandering. The mothers of the dead wore their sorrow as generals their golden collars, and the death of the fallen became a kind of decoration for the bereaved. But even the relatives of heroes who were engaged in quite safe duties were as proud as if they had a dead man to mourn, and the nuances between mothers of the deceased and mothers of the living were effaced in the familiar general 'gravity of the times'. Since all alike was tragic, all imagined themselves as making a sacrifice.

Already appeals for the first War Loan were posted on every wall, alongside notices of the third call-up. The portrait-painter was in uniform, even if a fanciful one hastily invented by some military official. There had not been adequate preparations for artists to participate in the war. The war propaganda department could not cope with so many painters and writers, historians and journalists, dramatists and drama critics. The journalists wore leather gaiters and revolvers and an arm-band on which the word 'Press' was stitched in gold letters. The drama critics went into the archives and were allowed to wear civilian clothes so as not to have to appear as NCO's. The painters were left to their own devices. They made portraits of the army leaders, painted the walls of military hospitals in gay and cheerful colours, and wrote diaries or letters which they then published as the 'guests of Literature'. They too went for medical examinations, but usually had a number of disorders that kept them from the shooting. Some of the dramatists began to write regimental histories.

At Herr von Maerker's house, where Hilde acted as mediator between literature, art and the history of art, there gathered not only fighting men but also painters and writers. Friedrich found their glances curious and quizzing. His revolutionary opinions and his Siberian experiences, together with his readiness to struggle against Tsarism – which people took for granted – fitted in with their conception of the identity of freedom and the cause of the Fatherland. His very presence attested to this identity.

The writer G., one of the cultivated satirists who knew how to combine a decadent manner, elegant posturing and large debts with a sensitive feeling for language, was immersed in a discussion with young Baron K. about the French literature of the Enlightenment. He avoided the discussion of current events. He was, in fact, a sceptic and might have upset the general optimism. If he had expressed his opinions, it would have been all over with his congenial occupation and civilian clothing. However, in order not to appear as a man without any kind of attachment to the Fatherland, he said 'The war is the very time in which one is able to think. Never before have I been able to read so extensively and with so few distractions. At present I am reading the French. It affords me a special pleasure to get to know our enemies better. They are cruel and clever. The entire race is impelled by their so-called *"raison"*. It is quite obvious to me, of course, that such sound commonsense rears a thrifty lower middle class but not a heroic nation. Great occasions call for a sweet unreason.'

Hilde smiled and exchanged a glance with the writer. She understood that he had spoken for her and not to the lieutenant. She did not much care for the cavalry. For whereas the writer and the 'intellectuals' – this word was used increasingly often – discussed the very simplest battle reports in such a manner that nothing remained of their actuality but a faint echo, which Hilde found agreeable, the lieutenant named names, numbers, kilometres and divisions, which bored her. And although he said nothing that the others could not have said, had they wished to, it seemed as if he alone knew what war was all about.

Besides this lieutenant, Hilde's father alone among all the men present remained an object for her particular disdain. Only since the war had the ministerial adviser participated in his daughter's entertainments, so changed was he by the great event. Among all the groups of that social class which produced no officers, no ministerial officials, no diplomats and no landed proprietors, the one he most detested consisted of what he called the 'Bohemians', of whom his notions were infantile. Even now when, revolutionized by wartime enthusiasm, he yielded to the general illusion that differences would be abolished and that a painter in travelling clothes and riding-breeches who painted a base hospital and a base commandant was part of the baggage-train of heroes, even now he winced imperceptibly when the painter P., as soon as anything exciting was mentioned, took his foot in his hands as if this manipulation was a necessary aid to better hearing, or when the drama critic R., in a quiet moment, broke a match between his teeth. In this unsuspecting state, which he owed to a secluded youth in a feudal institution, Herr von Maerker did not understand that these men did not display the free ways of an artistic disposition but the miserable ones of a lower middle-class upbringing. He regarded it as a method of expressing the artistic temperament.

Friedrich looked around. The war correspondent who had just returned from the front was talking with a lieutenant, a lawyer in mufti, about the excellent equipment of the troops. He wanted next to go to Belgium and describe the victory parade. A Liberal deputy, middle-aged and at that time not liable for service, was explaining to a one-year volunteer, to whom it was of no concern, that the war would constitute the final overthrow of clericalism and that non-denominational schools would come about in a matter of weeks. The ironic author was now talking to Hilde. He had left the young cavalryman sitting in silence, and although their chairs were touching the literary man was separated from the officer by a whole world, a world that abounded with French writings of the Enlightenment. The writer now wore round his mouth a smile that could be put on and taken off like a moustache-trainer, one that he used to make an impression on women. His suit, his deportment, his hairstyle, were the careful work of an entire morning. Out of sceptical protest he wore his elegant civilian suit, for which he had a special permit in his pocket. But it was as provocative as an injustice in contrast with the entire uniformed world. The painstakingness revealed by the knot of his necktie alone was a demonstration against the confusion of a whole epoch. The glance, full of gentle appraisal, with which he followed Hilde's gestures and seemed to note them behind his forehead, held the melancholy renunciation of a critical genius who had yielded to the censor and was compelled to conceal deep within himself the many witticisms that occurred to him at every communiqué from the front. Friedrich hated him even more than the painter.

He looked at Hilde. A slight flush, which darkened the brown of her cheeks, disclosed that she felt herself to be the centre of a circle of the elect who adored her and whom she herself venerated, and Friedrich asked himself if there was a causal connection between the adoration that pleased her and the veneration she rendered in return. She seemed strange and remote and almost hostile to him in the midst of these others. He would have liked to extract the immediate significance of every movement she made in order to detach her from her connection with this world, and the meaning of every word she said so that her beloved voice might continue as nothing but an innocuous sound. He loved her voice, but not her words. He loved her eyes, but hated what they recorded.

12

It was not until August that the Ukrainian P. returned from the camp. In the meantime it had become known that the Russian revolutionaries had for some time been the natural allies of the Central Powers. P.'s liberation from the camp was doubtless politically motivated. He remained in Vienna, the authorities were aware of it and even supported him. Some days after P.'s return Friedrich set out on his journey through Germany to Zürich. P. had been in contact with Zürich throughout, even during his stay in the camp, and with Comrade Tomkin in M. in Brandenburg – one of the middlemen between the comrades and the secret police. He was unchanged. Robust and carefree as he was, he seemed to regard the years up to the war, the straits in which he always lived and his sufferings in the concentration camp, as a kind of necessary gymnastic exercise, which he was able to surmount. He was unafraid, not because he was brave but because the bulk and strength of his muscles, the inexhaustible elasticity of his tendons and nerves and a healthly abundance of red blood left no room for fear. He was as little capable of being afraid as a tree. But, like every fearless man, he understood that anxiety did not always flow from cowardice but was also a quality connected with one's physical constitution and nerves.

'Your worrying was unnecessary,' said P. to Friedrich. 'If you'd been locked up, they'd soon have let you out. We are allies for the time being and under the protection of a powerful institution. Our comrades even receive passports. You'll be taken care of too. You will now go to M., here is an address. You will report to this man and he'll give you money and papers for Switzerland. Give my greetings to the comrades. I'm staying here for the moment. I might be able to cross the lines to Russia.'

He said 'cross the lines to Russia' as if it were a matter of going for a pleasant drive. He had decided to make a rendezvous with the comrades as one arranges an excursion to a well-known and popular beauty spot. He sat, powerful and calm on his old sofa which was wide and large enough for a grown man but seemed narrow, short and fragile under the weight and force of his body.

'In order to avoid any unpleasantness just now, you will travel first class,' said P. 'You'll find yourself in the good society of higher officers and war contractors and no policeman will dare to demand your identity card. But if it should happen, make a fuss and snarl at any officials who cross your path.'

They walked slowly through the streets. P. had the solemn deliberation of a burgomaster. 'If one has my kind of appearance,' he said, 'no one in Central Europe will be the least bit suspicious. The Germans, and the smaller races within the German cultural sphere, have an indestructible trust in broad shoulders. Compare, for instance, the popularity of Hindenburg with the anonymity of Hötzendorf, who is small and elegant. The Russians command respect, although they are enemies. But the Russian generals have broad epaulettes, like the Germans. Striplings like yourself evoke mistrust.'

In order to see Friedrich safely on his way, P. accompanied him to the station. And with the joviality that sprang from his nature, he delivered Friedrich into the care of the conductor. 'My dear fellow,' he said, 'my friend is ill and must have agreeable neighbours.' 'Thank you, Excellency,' said Friedrich, so loudly that the policeman who was due to accompany the train must have heard. 'Take care of yourself,' said P. and bade him farewell. The conductor and the policeman saluted as P. left the platform with great strides.

Friedrich was not left alone in the compartment. A German colonel and an Austrian major climbed in. They

116

exchanged greetings. It was wartime and one could be sure that no common travellers sat in the first class. Nowadays, whoever got on the train and wore civilian clothes was even mightier than a uniform. Clever officers, therefore, had gradually accustomed themselves to regard civilians they encountered in the first class as superiors.

They were the more resentful when, just before the train departed, the conductor squeezed in one more passenger who would have made a more suitable first-class passenger in peacetime. Both officers exchanged a quick glance. While the eyebrows of each were raised in astonishment, their moustaches were already smiling. Both moved nearer each other as if they now had to join in mutual defence. The passenger so suspiciously received did not seem to notice anything for the moment. He sat very free and comfortable because the others had made themselves so small. He was shortsighted, as was betrayed by the thick lenses of his pince-nez, the way his head was permanently poked forwards, and his uncertain searching movements. He had evidently been in a hurry not to miss the train, his panting was clearly audible. His short legs dangled slightly above the floor, continually sought by the tips of his toes. His plump white hands lay on his knees and his fingers drummed inaudibly on the soft material of his trousers.

A black goatee in which the first grey hairs sprouted gave the gentleman the appearance of a high banking official. 'A pimp!' Friedrich heard the German colonel whisper. 'Army rabbi!' whispered the Austrian major.

The man whose vocation was not yet definitely established was meanwhile gazing affably and cordially at his fellow-passengers. His panting had gradually stopped. It was clear that he was satisfied with his present situation.

Finally he stood up, bowed slightly, first to the colonel, then to the major, and lastly – but only with a slight nod – to Friedrich. 'Doctor Süsskind,' he said out loud. His voice conveyed more assurance than his body.

'You're probably enlisting as an army chaplain, your reverence?' said the Austrian major, while a shadow fell over the face of the silent colonel. 'No!' said the man, who had sat down again in the corner with feet dangling. 'I am a war correspondent.' And he gave the name of a Liberal newspaper. 'Ah – war correspondent?' said the major.

'I was recently in your country, touring the Austro-Hungarian monarchy,' replied the correspondent authoritatively.

'Well, I hope everything turned out to your liking,' said the major lightly and indifferently.

'Not everything, unfortunately!' began the journalist. 'I had the opportunity of talking with several important personalities and with clever men not in office. It seemed to me, in Austria' – he corrected himself, with an emphatic bow in the direction of the German colonel – 'with our allies, that a stronger central driving force was needed. The organization leaves much to be desired. The Austrian is sanguine and the nations he rules are still uncivilized. It would also be as well to impose a little silence on the different national demands as long as we are fighting. Yes, gentlemen!'

What countries had he seen? asked the major.

'The Poles, among others,' replied the correspondent. In Cracow he had eaten well but slept badly from fear of vermin. And in Budapest he had seen two bugs in one night. The Hungarians refused to speak German to him. Yet they understood everything. A lieutenant of hussars had been very charming but had had no idea of the importance of the artillery on the Western Front. Yes!

'There are lice at the front,' said the Austrian major, as if he intended to tell quite another story. But he said no more.

In Pressburg, related the journalist, he had heard how soldiers in a tavern had spoken a Slav dialect. 'It must have been Slovak,' he stated, 'with a German word now and again.'

'Perhaps it was Czech,' said the major.

'Could be,' replied the reporter, 'but isn't it all the same?' Even Czech wasn't so very different.

'A Bavarian can't understand a Prussian,' remarked the major.

'You're mistaken!' said the newsman excitedly. 'They are only dialects.' And he began to praise the unity of all German strains, not taking his eyes off the German colonel the while. The latter looked out of the window.

Suddenly the colonel turned round and said : 'Talking of dialects, you are from Frankfurt, aren't you?'

'No! From Breslau!' retorted the correspondent in a firm, almost military, voice.

'Not bad either,' said the colonel and regarded the landscape anew.

'So you are from the press,' began the Austrian major, as if he had only just realized that the reporter had something to do with a newspaper. 'The seventh great power, eh?' he enquired amiably.

The journalist smiled. 'Now,' continued the major, 'you know better than we do when it will end. What's your opinion?'

'Who can tell!' replied the journalist. 'Our armies are deep in enemy territory. The nation is united as never

119

before. The Social Democrats are fighting like everyone else. Who would have thought this miracle possible! You are on your way to Germany, aren't you? Well, you'll see how all our distinctions of class and creed have vanished. The old dispute between Catholicism and Protestantism is over.'

'Really,' said the major. 'Well, and how about the Israelites?'

The journalist was silent and the colonel smiled at the landscape.

'A dwindling number!' said the bearded one, as if he would have liked to say: 'There aren't any at all.'

'Our Israelites are very brave,' continued the major perseveringly.

'Excuse me,' said the journalist and left the compartment. They saw him through the glass of the door. He went right and then left.

'Occupied!' intimated the colonel. And, as if the occupied W.C. were a matter of geography, he said: 'He's from Breslau.'

When the correspondent sat down in his place again he began to talk about Paris at the outbreak of war, where he had been working for several years for his newspaper. He spoke at length about the measures the Parisians had taken against the Germans, who were destined to be sent off to camps. Often and again he mentioned the names of the German ambassador, some military attachés and embassy counsellors. He seemed to wish to attribute a special significance to the fact that he had left the country in the same train in which the staff of the German embassy had travelled. And some ten times in his narrative he returned to the phrase: 'We, a dozen German gentlemen'. The colonel continued to look out at the landscape.

A German delegation which had left the enemy country at the same time as Dr Süsskind meant less to him than the troop kitchen of a foreign regiment. It was easy for the reporter to talk of military attachés. The Austrian major paid no more attention. He drew out a notebook and asked: 'Do you know any Jewish jokes, Doctor?' And as the correspondent did not reply the major began reading out jokes from his notebook, which all began with the words: 'Two Jews were sitting in a train.' The colonel regarded the major with a despairing and reproachful seriousness. The journalist had assumed a fixed smile to oblige, which became neither more nor less marked but remained the same at the point of the jokes as at their beginning. And only Friedrich laughed. Once, when the major used one of those Yiddish expressions that had already become part of the German vocabulary of wags and tailors, which he could reasonably assume everyone present would understand, the interested journalist asked what it meant. 'What, you don't know what it means?' asked the major. 'No.' The correspondent claimed not to know. Only gradually did he recall that once, on a journey through Egypt, he had heard a similar sounding Turkish word. And he mentioned Egypt as if that country had never played an important part in the history of his race. The colonel redoubled his attentions to the window-pane, as if the landscape had become even more interesting.

They were nearing the German frontier. The major had finished his jokes. He was turning the pages in his little book in the hope of finding a hidden anecdote. But he found no more.

The journalist became restless, got up, and lifted his case from the luggage-rack with a visible effort.

'Are you getting out?' asked the colonel, without look-

ing up and in a tone that he might have used to say:
'Have we got rid of you?'

'Yes, indeed, Colonel!' came the firm and soldierly
reply.

As the train travelled more slowly and the first signs of
an approaching station became evident, the journalist put
his case in the corridor, returned to the compartment,
clicked his heels together with a snap one would not have
credited him with and said goodbye.

To the ire of the Prussian colonel, the Austrian major
held out his hand and said: 'It's been a pleasure!'

The colonel contented himself with saying: 'Likewise!'
It sounded like an oath.

The journalist stood on the platform and embraced his
wife. She was wearing a wide black feathered hat which
sat flat as a saucer on her head. Her large red ears were
aflame in the cold. In her hand she carried an umbrella
with a yellow handle of twisted horn.

The train started to move off again slowly.

13

'So that's the newspaper correspondent Süsskind,' thought
Friedrich. He knew the name and the newspaper in which
this man's initials figured so often and so prominently.
No connection could be found between the style that
singled out this correspondent from his colleagues and
the servility with which he denied his Jewishness. 'This

Süsskind,' said the colonel, as if he meant to pursue Friedrich's thoughts aloud, 'would do better to stay out of sight.'

The train was delayed; it did not arrive at M. until the early morning.

M. was a small town in which it was raining. Most of the houses were built of dark red brick. In the middle of the town was a green square, and in the middle of the square rose a steep red-brick building. It was a Protestant church.

Opposite the entrance to the church stood a school for boys and girls, made of red brick. To the right of the school stood a revenue office of red brick. And to the left of the school was the town hall with a pointed spire. It too was made of red brick.

In the wide shop-windows were leather goods made of paper, wristwatches for soldiers, cheap novels, and mittens for Christmas in the field.

From inside the boys' and girls' school came the sound of clear children's voices singing : *In der Heimat, in der Heimat.* From time to time a dark-green tramcar glided by rapidly, swaying and emanating a brisk clanging. And it rained, heavily, slowly, monotonously from a deep dark-grey leaden sky that had not been blue for a single hour since the creation of the world.

It rained. Friedrich found a seat in a large empty café on whose wide windows were posted patriotic and puristic notices such as : 'Don't say *adieu* but *auf Wiedersehn!*' and 'Don't use foreign languages!', alongside picture postcards with verses by Theodor Körner in heavy type. A waitress brought him a pallid coffee with a pinkish tinge at the edges. He sat by the window and watched the rain trickling down. It struck twelve from the town

123

hall, and the girl workers and a few isolated workmen emerged from the munitions factory. They were a silent crowd. Only their steps could be heard on the damp cobbles. Even the young girls did not speak. They walked at the head of the irregular file because they had nimbler legs than the others. He had plenty of time. Tomkin was not available before five in the afternoon.

Friedrich got into a tram. It was empty. A conductress sold him his ticket. She had left her ears exposed and done up her hair so tightly at the nape of her neck that she could have been taken for a man. A tin trumpet hung at her bosom like a brooch. The poor woman wore pince-nez. She walked with long strides through the swaying car like old sea-dogs on deck in a tempest. As no one was sitting in the car, Friedrich asked her if she would not sit down. She directed her pince-nez at him and said: 'Conductors aren't allowed to.' Friedrich felt offended by the masculine plural in which she had so firmly included herself. And, irritated, he said to her: 'You're no conductor!' using the masculine form. 'I'd have you know,' she replied, pince-nez directed straight at him, 'that you have committed an offence against an official. I shall report you!' 'In this town,' Friedrich thought, 'Babel had lived. Women and Socialism. This country is the home of the proletarian idea. Here the proletariat is most strongly organized.'

The conductress continued to walk to and fro as if she had passengers to look after. 'She will report me!' thought Friedrich. And, although he now had cause enough to avoid any encounter with the authorities, he decided to stay in the tram.

The tram reached the terminus. He remained seated. The conductress went up to him and said: 'Get out!'

'I'm going back again!' said Friedrich. 'Then you must buy another ticket!' 'Obviously!'

'It's not obvious at all,' said the conductress. 'I can let you travel back again even without a ticket.' And once again the pince-nez stared straight at him.

'Be friendly to me!' he begged. 'I'm on duty!' she retorted.

He travelled once more through the entire town. No one got in.

'Do you always have so few passengers?' he asked. 'Fares!' she corrected him, without answering the question.

He was finally reduced to silence. He looked through the dirty windows, read the posters, the call-up notices. At last he got out and sat down again in the café. He was brought a beer without being asked.

And it rained.

He asked for paper and wrote a letter to Hilde. It was one of the most remarkable love-letters that have ever been written. It ran as follows:

'Most gracious and esteemed Fräulein, I did not speak the truth when I told you that I should be enlisting next week. I shall never enlist. I am on my way to Switzerland. I did not have the opportunity to tell you what I feel about this war; I shall not even try. You know enough of my life to realize that I am no coward. If I tell you that I shall not enlist to fight for your Franz Joseph, the French war industry, the Tsar, Kaiser Wilhelm, it is not because I fear for my life but because I wish to preserve it for a better war. I shall await its outbreak in Switzerland. It will be a war against society, against the fatherlands, against the poets and painters who come to your house, against cosy family life, against the false authority of the father and the false obedience of the children, against progress and against your "emancipation", in a word against the bourgeoisie. There are others besides who will fight with me in this war. But not many who have been so well prepared for it by their private destiny. I should certainly have hated the family, even if I had known one. I should certainly have mistrusted patriotic catchwords even if I had been reared in love of my country. But my conviction has become a passion because I am what in your vocabulary is called "stateless". I shall go to war for a world in which I can be at home.

'I send you this avowal only because I have to follow it with another, which is that I love you. Or – because I mistrust the ideas the bourgeois vocabulary supplies us with and the words so often misused in your society – I believe that I love you. When I saw you that first time in the carriage, you were so to speak part of a goal I was not yet fully familiar with but which I had nevertheless set myself. You were one of the aims towards which I was striving. I intended to conquer the power within the society to which you belonged. But the impotence of this society has been revealed to me earlier than I might then have thought. Even if I did not have the conviction that one must annihilate a rotten world, even if I were merely an egoist, I could not continue to strive for a power that is only a fiction. Although my aim today differs from the one of which you once seemed to me to form a part, I have never ceased to think of you. I should like to forget you, and indeed have had opportunity enough to do so. That I cannot do so seems to me a proof that I love you.

'I should therefore really strive to win you. But then it would first be necessary for one of us to convert the other. And that is impossible. I shall therefore, as they say, renounce you. I confess that I tell you this in the very vague hope that you might sometime give me occasion, not to find renunciation unnecessary, but at least to regret it. And in this so indefinite and yet so comforting hope I kiss your hands, for which I yearn.

Farewell!

Your Friedrich'

At five he went to meet Tomkin.

He was one of those revolutionaries whom R. called 'harsh ascetics'. A tailor by calling and of a dogged faith. 'I've been living here for five years,' he announced. 'And you like it here?' asked Friedrich, and he thought of the rain, the factory, the conductress, the café. Tomkin did not understand the question. Perhaps he is hearing it for the first time, thought Friedrich. 'I found work here!' Tomkin answered at last, as if he had only just arrived at the sense of the question. And, as if statistics formed part of the answer, he continued: 'Eight thousand workers live here, all in Red organizations, you can rely on them. The unions are alright. Four thousand women are organized, including the conductresses and municipal auxiliaries.'

'Really!' said Friedrich.

'This war is leading to the Revolution,' said the tailor. 'You know that as well as I do, don't you, comrade? We have much to expect from the German proletariat,' he continued. 'Even though it has gone to war?' asked Friedrich. 'An act of the party bosses!' said the tailor. 'One of them lives here. I've got to know him. When I told him you were coming, he begged me to bring you to him. Will you see him?' 'Take me to him!' said Friedrich.

He was one of those men whose patriotic speeches since the outbreak of war were quoted in the bourgeois French and English newspapers as evidence of the downfall of proletarian solidarity and the triumph of national sentiment.

He lived in three rooms, whose furniture had been gradually accumulated, piece by piece, each one newer than the other. The two sons of the house had joined up. Their photograph, showing them arm-in-arm in uniform, stood in a frame with pale-blue forget-me-not ornamentation on the father's desk. At either side of the large mirror, which hung between two windows like a third, but reflecting the light of the room and not that of the street, hung two paintings depicting the harvest and a red sunset, one of a farmer with scythe flying over thick golden ears of corn, another of three women bent over binding sheaves. A small fragile table displayed so-called knick-knacks, a chimney-sweep of blue porcelain and a lucky mascot of red clay in the form of a pig, a doll's kitchen with tiny pots and pans, a shepherd playing the flute, the photograph of a bearded man in a broad red plush frame with the same pale-blue forget-me-not ornaments which decorated the frame of the soldiers' photograph. An enormous inkstand reposed on the desk. It was of metal, a bronze knight in full array held his shield horizontally like a tray so that pen-nibs could be placed on it. Two little pots at either side with small cupolas attached to iron lids, held ink, one red, the other blue. A bronze paperknife lay alongside. It was shaped like a sabre. The chairs were hard, despite being upholstered.

He was a fine fellow who had worked his way up through diligence and a creditable lack of original ideas.

He had maintained a happy marriage with one and the same woman from his twenty-first year, partly by following the advice of a popular nature-cure doctor. He was a fine fellow with a slight hint of a belly and with simple features that a child might have traced. He helped his guests to cigars from a box, from whose lid the German and Austrian emperors looked out into the world, red-cheeked and cheerful, framed by a small gold-rimmed oval.

'In Zürich, comrade,' he said to Friedrich, 'you'll see how the world treats us. People can't get over our invasion of Belgium. I was against it from the start. But the war has quickly taught us to distinguish the solid basis of fact from theory. In peacetime it's a different matter. One can make claims in a flourishing economy. But if the entire economy is imperilled one must try to preserve it, whether one is an employer or an employee. I know that you and your comrades don't share our opinions. But it's easier for you. You simply can't compare us, proletarians but with equal civil rights as citizens of a western, civilized, constitutional monarchy, with the oppressed Russian proletariat. It is clear that the Russian proletarian is no patriot in the sense that the German proletarian is. After the war our Kaiser will have to be contented with a purely decorative role, like the King of England for example. A victory for the Tsar would lead only to greater oppression of the Russian proletariat, a German victory to the liberation of the German. Then we shall take giant strides towards the Republic.'

Friedrich took his leave before midnight, when he heard the party leader's wife calling from the bedroom. It was still raining. The town was dark. Not a single one of its many windows showed a gleam of light. The people slept in the midst of war. Was there no widow mourning her husband? Could mothers sleep whose sons had fallen? He recalled the night when he had walked through the streets of Vienna. Then, too, all were asleep with few exceptions. Those who had woken then were now in the field, in concentration camps, in prisons or, at best, in Switzerland. The others slept. They slept when it was still peacetime and the war was only getting under way, they were sleeping now. 'Today, as then, I am the only un-sleeping being in the world. Each has his tomb, his grave, his stone with its inscription, his baptismal certificate, his documents, his military pass, his Fatherland. That gives them security. They can sleep. The codings in the chancellery offices register their fate. There is no govern-ment office in the world that has my coding. I have no number. I have nothing.'

In that town, and on that night, he was the only human being awake. He opened the window and looked out into the dark street. From the second floor on which his window lay he saw the feeble rectangular glimmer on the wall opposite and that gave him a certain satisfaction, as if the glimmer were his reward.

It was still raining.

It also rained the next two days, while he had to wait for his passport. 'The German authorities,' said the tailor consolingly, 'are even making conditions in places where they are themselves becoming illegal.'

'How quickly Kapturak manages it!' thought Fried-rich.

Nevertheless, he was delighted when he had the pass-port and the tailor handed him his travelling money. 'For the first time,' he said to himself, 'I have proper documents. The authorities themselves have become my accomplices. Such are the miracles of war. Things are progressing.'

The next day he travelled to Zürich.

He sat in the third class and listened to the soldiers talking. They spoke of quite ordinary things: of bacon, meat dishes, a medical officer, a field hospital, brands of cigarettes. They had already domesticated the war. They were already living at their ease. The violent and premature death that was now stalking them had become as familiar as natural death in times of peace, familiar and remote. The war, once an unnatural phenomenon, had become a natural one.

At the last station before the frontier, he put Hilde's letter in the post. 'By the time it reaches her, I'll be over there.'

He telegraphed his arrival to Berzejev.

14

From that moment he thought only of Berzejev. He would be seeing him soon. He remembered the origin of this friendship. Even more easily recalled than troubles suffered in common and dangers endured together during their escape, were Berzejev's words and gestures, fixed in Friedrich's memory without any particular association. He remembered how Berzejev slept and how he ate, how he held his left knee between his hands when he sat down and was pensive, and how he used to wash himself in the morning, rapidly and carefully and with a visible enjoyment of cold and water that was like a daily reaffirmation of the union of man with the elements.

He was already travelling over Swiss soil. No more martial posters on the station walls and no more trains full of uniformed men. It was as if he had come straight from a battle, not just from a country at war. Only here did the peaceful world he had yearned for in Siberia begin. It seemed to him that peace held a strange and unfamiliar aspect and that war had been the more obvious and natural condition. Throughout the entire journey across Russia, Austria and Germany he had grown accustomed to the idea of the sovereignty of certain death in Europe. All of a sudden, at a frontier, ordinary life began. It was as if he had reached the edge of a downpour and had been allowed to glimpse briefly how sharp the separation was between blue and cloudy sky, damp and dry earth. Suddenly he saw young men in civilian clothes who should long ago have worn uniform. Suddenly he saw men tranquilly taking their leave of women, heard how they said to each other : 'Till we meet again'. It was evident that all were secure in their lives. At the newsstands the newspapers of every country hung side by side, as if they did not contain reports of bloodshed. 'So this is the substance of neutrality, he told himself. 'Even from the train I can feel how unimportant the war is. The awareness that so much blood is flowing no longer fills everyone's thoughts. I begin to understand the disinterestedness of God. Neutrality is a kind of divinity.'

'He'll be at the station,' he said. And, immediately afterwards, 'He won't come to the station, he'll wait for me at the house. There's no point in waiting for someone at the station. Besides, so far I've always arrived alone.

No one has ever expected me or accompanied me. All the same, I shall be pleased if he is at the station.'

But Berzejev really was waiting, placid as ever. 'You got my telegram, then?' asked Friedrich. 'No,' said Berzejev, 'I've been meeting every train coming from Germany for a week.' 'But whom were you expecting?' 'You!' said Berzejev.

For the first time they saw each other in European civilian clothes. For the first time each noticed in the other's dress a few minor features that were like the ultimate and most irrefutable evidence of the community of their way of thought. 'So you're wearing your hat, then!' said Friedrich. 'You don't like it?' asked Berzejev. 'On the contrary, I can't picture it otherwise.' And they talked like two young men of the world about neckties, hats, double-breasted and single-breasted coats, as if there were no war and as if they were not there to await the Revolution.

'If Savelli could hear us!' said Berzejev, 'how he'd despise us. Even here he obstinately insists on going around without a collar, to spite us, to spite R. and myself, and especially all "intellectuals". It's no ordinary ostentation. With him, it's real hatred.'

As a matter of fact things weren't going well for any of them. They had nothing to live on. It was a struggle for them to raise enough money each week for the flat. Savelli ate only once a day, R. urgently needed a pair of trousers. He wrote for a review, for which Savelli despised him. 'And you?' asked Friedrich. 'I have money,' said Berzejev. 'I'm working. I've found work at a theatre. An actor I've become friendly with got a place for me. It wasn't easy. The Swiss theatrical employees were not friendly at first; finally they found me congenial. I've even

133

saved money. We could both live for a month without lifting a finger. You're staying at my place. No rooms available. Deserters and pacifists have occupied the whole of Switzerland.'

And they resumed their old life.

15

In Zürich Friedrich began to keep a proper diary. I reproduce below those of its passages that seem to me important.

From Friedrich's diary :

'I met R. again today. He was the same as ever. He spoke to me as if we had parted only yesterday. I remembered exactly our last conversation before my departure to Russia. But naturally he had forgotten it. It's thanks to him that I decided to write this diary. "What?" he said, "you're not keeping notes? Wrong! First it is a manifestation of individuality. Pencil in hand, a sheet of white paper in front of me. From a small piece of paper, not to mention a large sheet, there emanates a stillness and a solitude. A desert could not be more tranquil. Sit down with an empty notebook in a noisy café – you are at once alone. Second, it's practical, because there are various things one shouldn't forget. Third, a diary is a safeguard against the all too hectic activity to which our calling condemns us, as it were. It helps us to distance events. Fourth, I write because Savelli would despise it as bourgeois sentimentality if he knew about it."

'I, too, have a natural propensity for things that Savelli terms bourgeois sentimentality. I have met him again. Not a word about Siberia. Not a word about my escape. Only : "Berzejev tells me things have gone very well for you." And it seemed for a moment as if I ought to demand pardon because I had been arrested. For the first time I have become really convinced that he hates me, at those times when he does not despise me too greatly. He repeated to me what Berzejev had already said : it would have been better if we had both remained in Russia. There was more to do there. I could not restrain myself from telling him that Russia was not, in fact, my home. "So much the worse!" he replied. It was a striking demonstration of nationalism. At that moment I felt like a European, as it were, just as R. terms himself. He means the great European traditions : Humanism, the Catholic Church, the Enlightenment, the French Revolution and Socialism. He said recently that Socialism was a concern of the West and that it would be as foolish to speak of Socialism in Russia as of Christianity to Hottentots. R. might be my older brother. We probably have more in common than qualities alone. It seems to me that we share a similar destiny. We are both sceptics. We both hate the same things. We want the Revolution for the same reasons. We are both cruel. It is laid down that we shall prepare a revolution but probably not experience its victorious outcome. I cannot believe, any more than he, that anything in the world will change except nomenclature. We hate society, personally, privately, because it happens not to please us. We hate the fat and bloody cosiness in which it lives and dies. Had we been born in a previous century we should have been reactionaries, possibly priests, lawyers, aides-de-camp, anonymous secretaries in a European court. We ought both to have been born in an age when extraordinary men could still determine their own fate, while average men remained insignificant.

'A week ago I took the place of the correspondent of a Danish radical newspaper. My duties are to take an interest in society, politics, the theatre; and I believe that I do my work well. "You have," says R., who secured me this job as a correspondent, "the first quality of a journalist : you are curious."

'The deserters who live here are not to be distinguished from the pacifists. None of those fortunate enough to have crossed the frontier admits that he fled from a private love for life. As if love for life needed any excuse! It is an attribute of the middle classes to conceal the simple necessities of nature behind complicated ideals. The men of past times might lose their life in a stupid duel. But they died for their personal honour and did not deny for a moment that life was dear to them. The men of today, at least most of the men now to be found in neutral countries, allege that they are the victims of their convictions.

'I am interested above all in those who have come to Switzerland with the permission of their own countries. In fact, one can learn most from them. They come here to spy on the pacifists of their own countries and to make official propaganda for their ideals. There are two living in our boarding-house, a German and a Frenchman. The German's name, ostensibly, is Dr Schleicher, the Frenchman's Bernardin. That they sit at my table for breakfast is due to the naïvety of our landlady. The landlady believes that the two have something in common because of their pacifist ideas, and find pleasure in eating at the same table, two poor victims of their fatherlands. Instead of which, each is the paid spy of his country. Dr Schleicher is a decent, easygoing man. He gets up late, goes to the toilet in slippers and dressing-gown, and stays there a very long time. He wears glasses, which make his eyes friendly, his broad face even broader, and which lie like a second gold-rimmed glassy smile over the permanent natural smile of his cheeks. Whenever I go by his door I hear a machine clattering. He is a naïve spy, who believes one to be convinced that he is not writing reports for his superiors, but typing love-letters. Bernardin is a man in his forties. He has the solemn sombre elegance of a provincial Frenchman who looks every day as if he were going to a funeral; only the cheerful expression with which he awaits his meals softens his solemnity. His shoes are always shiny and often covered by dark-grey spats, his trousers are always creased, his jacket looks as if it had just come from the tailor, his high stiff collar is always white and glossy. He continually strokes his small black moustache, which emphasizes the brownish-red of his cheeks, with two thoughtful fingers. He wears small bow-ties, as if in a conscious demonstration against the heavy silk knitted neckties of Dr Schleicher. Neither says a word to the other. They acknowledge each other smilingly and silently when they sit down and when they get up. They know about each other. Only the Frenchman writes his reports by hand, and it is quiet when one passes his door.

'Yesterday the German and the Frenchman conversed for the first time. They very nearly did not come to eat at all. They remained together for a long time after everyone was ready, they drank coffee and smoked. I was curious as usual. I know Dr Schleicher from the café, we have a mutual acquaintance, Dr Gold. This Dr Gold has not yet decided which side to take among the warring countries. He has lived a long time in Germany and in France and, from fear that one of the two countries might possibly win and that he might learn of it too late, he remains neutral. He sometimes sits at Dr Schleicher's table, sometimes at Bernardin's. He is on good terms with both. He reports on the one to the other. From fear that one day both might turn on him, he has been trying for months to bring them together. Yesterday he finally succeeded. He told me the course of events as follows: "Unfortunately, it occurred to me yesterday," said Dr Gold, "to say to Dr Schleicher that Bernardin had been wanting for a long time to make his acquaintance. And then I discovered that they sit together at table every day. I was in despair. If I were not as adept as I am, I should have blamed myself. But with my innate aplomb, I replied coolly: 'Then he cannot know with whom he has the honour of sitting at table.' And Dr Schleicher believed it. Only he happens to find Bernardin extremely uncongenial, and not only on grounds of nationality. And now I made my second mistake. 'He is, after all, a man of the law,' I said to Schleicher, 'a pleasant man in civilian life. But the war goes to the heads of these people.' 'What? A lawyer?' asks Schleicher. 'But I too am a lawyer.' At that moment in came Bernardin and Schleicher was the first to greet him, all smiles. At last I've brought them together. And what do you know! In half an hour the two were as thick as thieves. They talked only of pupils and teachers!"

'So much for Dr Gold. He soon left me, as busy as ever. He talks breathlessly, almost panting, and always on the go. What's more, he whispers. And he takes care that everyone around sees how diligent he is in retailing secrets. He is continually being greeted and continually responding. He knows all the pacifists. He is a regular contributor to *European Peace*. Berzejev calls him the "freemason" in the jaunty manner in which he confuses freemasons with pacifists. The great extent of his stupidity is astonishing, combined as it is with a knowledge of literature, languages and countries, insignificant people and so-called personalities. He is credulous and takes every piece of information seriously, and considers everything he is told important. Obviously, he must be credulous to be able to tell another person anything with conviction.

'What is extraordinary and incomprehensible is the readiness of everyone to listen to him. But that seems to be a feature of most gregarious natures; they accept information from people as if from newspapers, as if the sound of a voice, the expression of a face and the character of the narrator were not much more important than what they have to say, as if his look might never have given the lie to his lips.

'Dr Schleicher and Bernardin are now always seen together. They evidently do not suspect that, in such proximity, they constitute a striking phenomenon, even for wartime Zürich. Beside Bernardin's ceremonial black, which gives him a resemblance to the manager of a large department store, Dr Schleicher's blond brightness suggests a sunny carefree holiday. The gold frame of his spectacles, the glittering glass, the sand-coloured overcoat, his tan shoes, his light-brown trousers, his brown bowler-hat and his pale face diffuse a lustre visible at a distance, and when he walks towards one he is like a stray piece of the sun, whereas the dark Bernardin at his side appears like a sort of long and narrow ray of darkness. They have gradually become the object of joking remarks even among the pacifists, whose surveillance has brought them here. But both the German and the Frenchman seem to feel the common nature of their calling more strongly than their difference of nationality. I have heard that the German teaches French and the Frenchman German. The governments of the belligerent states seem to regard a knowledge of the enemy's language as an adequate qualification for espionage and diplomacy. R. tells me that there is a shortage of spies, as there is of guns and bread and sugar, and that the employment of a legal official in secret diplomacy and in the press corps roughly corresponds to the employment of a Home Guard unit at the front.

'Every day one sees new faces. Again and again new refugees. The longer the war lasts, the stronger becomes the army of convinced or chance pacifists. Switzerland could deploy an immense foreign legion to defend its neutrality.

'Favourable news from Russia. A strike in Moscow, twenty-six factories at a standstill in the Ukraine. From Comrade P. a report that he has made every preparation to break through the front, as he calls it, and get to Russia. He asks for equipment. Someone must go and take it to him. I would gladly go. No one has money for the journey. Nothing can be sent by post because of the censorship. Tomorrow I shall go again to L. to fetch the equipment.

'I was with L. yesterday, for the third time now.

Plainly, things are worse and worse for him. He is ill at the moment, wears a thick coloured shawl round his neck and refuses to go to bed although he has been two weeks in an unheated room. He lodges with a decent chap whose respectability does not restrain him from punctually collecting the rent. T. was at L.'s. They were discussing an article that G. had just submitted. "He can't get away from metaphysics," complained L. "Why is he always on about God!" This was with not the least pleasure in blasphemy, such as I have often noticed with convinced atheists. Chaikin, for example, lived on terms of permanent hostility with God, and assumed an expression of sneering anxiety when he said the words : heaven, priest, church, God. When Berzejev jeers he looks like a boy who has lied to the catechists. He assumes an artful expression and reminds me of a street urchin who has pressed the knob of an electric doorbell to make a fool of the porter. It is as if he supposes that, because the door stays shut, there is really no porter there. I have also heard T. talk about religion. He treats God as an entrepreneur and a being with a mundane interest in the preservation of the existing order. However, scorn, like infantile jeers and serious antagonism, still seem to me to be confirmation of the existence of God. But L. scours out heaven with one little word so that one can almost hear its great emptiness. It is as if he had removed the clapper from a bell so that it swings soundlessly and without echo, still metal and yet the shadow of a bell. L. has the gift of removing obstacles with one hand, of opening vistas. He does not readily admit the possibility of surprises. "We must reckon with obstacles," he said, "but not with those that we cannot foresee. If we once allow ourselves to make allowances for incalculable contingencies, we shall lapse into the complacency that prevents us from wanting to see even those that are probable. We live on the earth. Our understanding is terrestrial. Supernatural forces do not intervene in earthly affairs. So why should we cudgel our brains over them! Only the possible exists on earth. And everything possible can be taken into account."

'L.'s secret lies in this deliberate limitation. I do not believe that he experiences emotion, hate, anger or love. He resembles a minor official. He has deliberately disciplined himself to inconspicuousness, and has probably used as much effort to this end as others do, for instance, to develop a significant profile. He lives in the cold. He suffers illness and want as an example to us. And the only affecting thing about him is his incognito. His beard is like an intentionally superfluous prolongation of his physiognomy. His skull is broad and white. His cheekbones are broad like his skull and his beard forms the black apex of a ghostly pale heart which has eyes and can see.

'I was in Vienna for two days. I travelled with our material and with L.'s commissions to P., on the eve of his "breakthrough". Otherwise I saw no one. I tried to speak to Grünhut. The Madame, as he always calls the midwife, told me with almost maternal pride that Grünhut really was rehabilitated. "Now he will at least have a beautiful death," she said, the handkerchief that a woman of her sort always has at hand in the same mysterious way that a bourgeois woman always mislays hers, already covering her eyes and with a soft sob in her voice. "The good Doctor!" "Perhaps he may still come back," I said in a slightly thoughtless attempt to comfort her. It became apparent that I had offered quite the wrong kind of comfort. "When anyone is as far away as he is," said the midwife, "they never come back. Besides I've let the room. Polish Jews live there now. Refugees." She uttered this word with a spiteful glassy brightness. "Dirty types, they don't join up, the man is quite free and both sons are unarmed Home Guards. I shall have to go on raising their rent. Don't you agree? Everything gets dearer and these people earn a lot of money!" In order not to have to listen to her further, I resorted to the death sentence she had passed on Grünhut. "You can safely keep the refugees," I said. "Grünhut will certainly perish." She produced the handkerchief once more. In wartime tears can also be an expression of hope.

'I have not written to Hilde. I have thought of her continually and haven't for a moment wanted to see her. If I had not undertaken to be sincere at all costs as soon as I sat down alone in front of this paper, shame would have prevented me from writing down that I have been to the photographer's show-case where a large portrait of Hilde had been on display for some time. It is not there any more. A lieutenant, in colour, now hangs in the window.

'Savelli now reveals an open hatred towards all of us. Only in L.'s room is he silent and discreet. L. curbs him by the very simple method of telling him the truth to his face, as if he were reading it to him out of a book. Even Savelli cannot accuse him of saying anything for private reasons. He has only convictions. "He is a phenomenal figure," says R. "He is loved, although he barely understands how to accept love. He is feared, although he has no power to spread fear. With him nature appears to be attempting an entirely new type of saint. A saint without a halo, without clemency and without the reward of

143

eternity. I find this sanctity rather chilling. Note how Savelli attempts to imitate L., and how he fails. He is simply a cold-blooded swine. He pretends to be someone who has killed personal interests. But he has them. Only his blood is so cold that his ambition appears like opinion and his hatred like good sense." Thus R.

'After being away from Zürich for two days, I no longer feel here the freedom of a neutral country. On the return journey I imagined the whole time that I should find everything changed, my friends and the crowded cafés and all the spies. I felt as if I were returning after ten years, although the days in Vienna had passed so quickly. The war has grown old, it becomes dull and sluggish and even resembles one of the many cripples it has produced. I no longer took any interest in my fellow-passengers because I believe I know exactly what they are thinking. If I were sitting in a compartment with Süsskind again today, I could prompt him in his opinions and play his role. Also those of the Prussian colonel and the Austrian major. I also know exactly what R. has to say, what Savelli and Berzejev assert. We live in this city like prisoners, not like escapees. This geographically limited neutrality seems like a prison now that the war has become geographically unlimited. It often occurs to me that we are afloat in a small boat, good and bad, decent people and scoundrels. And the journey has no end to it. Sometimes I wish that something terrible might happen, that Switzerland might declare war on someone and intern all of us or send us to the front. So much happens here and the air is filled with so-called items of news. But the events are always the same, and one victory is like another, one defeat like another, the enemy is like his enemy and the contestants are as little distinguishable as rifles. The events beat against our city, waves against a ship, always the same, always the same. And I write about them in the radical newspapers. When I read one of my sentences in print it sounds like the soft, peculiarly feeble echo of the idea I had intended to write down. When shall I ever be able to express it? I begin to doubt whether the war serves our ends, it simply cannot cease, it is too monstrous. It has outgrown earthly laws and speeds along like one of the heavenly bodies, obedient to the mysterious decree of an inertia that knows no end.'

16

Here we break off the quotations from Friedrich's diary. In any case, from now on his entries become increasingly rare. The diary now contains only news of a general nature which may in the meantime have acquired an historical value but does not interest us in this context. We know that his fear, expressed above, that the war would not come to an end proved false. It remains to report, however, that on a day of that memorable early spring of the year 1917, when the world began once again to alter its aspect, he left Switzerland. This was the period in which the rebellious Duma, in two short days, decided on the arrest of the Tsar. The intellectual revolutionaries and the workers demonstrated on the Nevski Prospekt. The first eighty-three dead of the Russian Revolution lay on the damp stones, and spilled into the melting heaps of snow, the Tsar took his last farewell of his weeping officers. Rodzianko, Goutshkov, Kerenski and Shipov took over power, Skoropadski placed himself at the disposal of the German Kaiser. The Russian general Lukomski dictated the deed of abdication at GHQ, General Alekrejev informed the entire Russian front that Russia had ceased to be a Tsardom and the historic railway train carried the leader of the definitive Russian Revolution through Germany to Petrograd. The Tsar was in Pskov. He received all the telegrams in which his army leaders declared their agreement with his abdication. And while Russia began to transform itself into a democratic republic, the man who was preparing the Soviet Republic was already living in the Tschesinka Hotel in Petrograd. The spring was changeable as ever, the snow melted, ran and froze again. Friedrich and Berzejev were working in Moscow. They had access to a weapons arsenal and every night, witnessed only by the bribed sentries, they conveyed to the factories a quantity of rifles and munitions covered with straw in small brisk carts.

For the second time – and just as when he used to traverse the border forest with Kapturak and the deserters – he imagined he could hear the cry of an entire people. He recalled the five deserters. They had stood still suddenly, like a commando, at the first light of day to take leave of their homeland. Where were they now? Cripples on the hard asphalt of American cities, murdered in the prisons of the world, withered to shadows by pestilence in concentration camps, persecuted by the police, or long rotted in graves. He recalled grey police quarters, narrow-browed clerks, the hard stony fists of sergeant-majors and the soft slimy hands of spies, four-edged bayonets, the pyramid of the bourgeois world, and public prosecutors under pictures of the Kaiser, the Magi of the ruling class. He heard the rattling sound of chains and the blaring brass of regimental bands. He saw the officers who passed through the zones of communication laced like the demi-mondaines of the war, and the painters in fantastic uniforms who painted heroic pictures of military commanders, the journalists, those soothsayers of the modern bourgeoisie, and the majors with their Jewish jokes, the midwives and the patriotically transformed Grünhuts, the beggars' canteen and Hilde's literary circle.

'We shall destroy this world!' he said to Berzejev. They rolled through the dark suburban streets, dressed as peasants coming from their villages to sell vegetables in the morning markets. The neatly packed rifles lay quietly in the straw. The two men saw the stars glittering cold and remote as ever, and felt the spring advancing as ever, and the wind that wafts it from the south-west like every other year. The horses' hooves struck an incessant display of sparks on the uneven cobblestones, kindled from the night and in the night expiring.

Book Three

The train took over eighteen hours to cover the short stretch between Kursk and Voronezh. It was a cold and clear winter's day. For a few niggardly hours the sun shone so strongly from a dark-blue, almost southern, sky that the men jumped out of the cold dark carriages at each of the frequent stopping-places, doffed their coats as if for some heavy work in the heat of summer, washed themselves with crunchy snow and dried off in the air and sun. In the course of this short day they had all acquired brown faces like folk in winter on the sportive heights of Switzerland. But twilight came suddenly and a sharp crystalline monotonous singing wind sharpened the dark cold of the long night and seemed incessantly to polish the frost, so that it became even more cutting and piercing. The windows of the coaches lacked panes. They had been replaced by boards, newspapers and rags. Here and there flickered a forlorn candle-stump, stuck on some chance metal projection on a wall or door, the purpose of which no one could any longer explain and which, paltry as it appeared, thanks to its very purposelessness recalled the long-lost luxury of trains and travel. There were first and third class coaches as it happened, coupled together, but all the passengers froze. Now and again someone stood up, took off his boots, blew inside them, rubbed his feet with his hands, and drew his boots on again carefully as if he wanted not to have to take them off again in the course of that night. Others considered it better to stand on tiptoe every few minutes and to make hopping movements. Each envied the other. Each thought his neighbour was better off, and the only remarks to be heard in the entire train were to do with the presumed goodness and warmth of this overcoat or that fur cap. Under the sleeves of a soldier a comrade had discerned grey and red striped mittens, whose origin even the owner himself could not account for. He swore that they were absolutely useless. One man, in his forties, with a wildly-grown red beard, reminiscent of a hangman, a satyr and a blacksmith all in one, but who two years before had run a peaceful grocery business, insisted on seeing the mittens. Since the Revolution, in which he had lost everything, he had wandered from one army to another until finally remaining with the Reds. He played the part of a much experienced man, a prophet who could foresee everything. He divined many things. With all his goodness of heart, he could live scarcely an hour without starting a quarrel. It seemed as if he found his own changeable existence tedious. The owner of the mittens was a shy peasant lad from the Tambov district, who would not hand them over out of embarrassment. Finally he had to submit to their removal by a neighbour who was a sailor, a jack-of-all-trades, a conjurer, a cook and a tailor, with the face of a provincial actor. The sailor knew about that kind of thing and declared that the English had invented mittens and human life resided entirely in the pulses. Consequently, as long as one protected them, one had no need to wear a fur. One after the other, they pulled on the scraps of wool and asserted that they really warmed like an oven. The sailor claimed to know that the girl who had presented these mittens to the lad from the Tambov district was an even better warming agent, and everyone asked if it were true.

The men who were just now discussing warmth came from the Siberian front, where they had beaten back the

Czech legionaries, and where they had hoped to stay longer and relax for a few weeks after a victory which was a decisive one in their eyes but which, in reality, signified only a provisional success. Instead of this, they had to go to the Ukraine, where the cold seemed crueller to them than in Siberia, even though their commandant, Comrade B., showed them with a thermometer in his hand that it did not reach more than 25 degrees below zero. The red-bearded one said there was nothing so unreliable as mercury. He himself had once had a fever and had a thermometer stuck in his mouth by a doctor. When he took it out it showed no more than 36 degrees, about as much as, say, a fish. However, the doctor had said that his pulse was too rapid for such a low temperature, and that might prove to be the case with the frost. Why did one have two or even three kinds of degrees of heat and cold? Because even the men of science were not at one over Celsius or Réaumur.

In fact, the troops froze more because they advanced slowly, had to retreat again, and because in the south they had to contend with better organized and more numerous enemy forces. Also they were still exhausted by the long journey, after which they were immediately thrown into the struggle again. The small war of movement had become as accepted by them as the great World War had once been, and just as they had lain patiently for months before the fortress of Przemysl or in the Carpathians, so they had now become familiarized with the short forced marches, the tedious railway journeys, the hurried digging of trenches, the assault on a village and the battle for a station, the hand-to-hand struggle in a church and the sudden shooting in the streets, squeezed in the shadow of a gateway. They knew what was in store for them tomorrow, as soon as they left the railway, but they did not think of the battle, only of thermometers and mittens, things in general and everyday events, politics and the Revolution. Yes, of the Revolution, which they discussed as if it concerned themselves very little, as if it was happening somewhere else, outside their ranks, and as if they were not at this very moment about to shed their blood for it. Only sometimes, when they got hold of one of the pamphlets or hurriedly produced newspapers, did they become aware that they themselves were the Revolution. In the entire train there was only one person who never for a moment forgot for what, and in whose name, he was fighting, and who told the soldiers so again and again; this was Friedrich.

After three long months, which seemed to him like years, he met up with Berzejev again in Kursk. 'Whenever I come across you again,' said Berzejev, 'you seem different to me! That was already the case when we had to separate repeatedly during our escape. One might say that you change your face even quicker than your name.' Since his return to Russia, Friedrich had borne the pseudonym under which he had published articles in the newspapers. He did not even confess to Berzejev that, in secret, he loved his new name like a kind of rank conferred by himself. He loved it as the expression of a new existence. He loved the clothing he now wore, the phrases that lay in his brain and on his tongue and which he untiringly uttered and wrote down; for he found a sensual pleasure in the very repetition. A hundred times already he had written the same things in the pamphlets. And each time it was his experience that there were certain words that never grew stale and were rather like bells that always produced the same sound, but also always a fresh awe because they hung so high above the heads of men. There were sounds not shaped by human tongues but which – borne by unknown winds in the midst of thousands of words of earthly speech – had been wafted from other-worldly spheres. There was the word : 'Freedom!' A word as vast as the sky, as unattainable by the human hand as a star. Yet created by the yearning of men who ever and again reached out for it, and drunk from the red blood of millions of dead. How many times already he had repeated the phrase : 'We want a new world!' And always the phrase was just as new as that which it expressed. And ever and again it fell like a sudden light over a distant land. There was the word : 'People.' When he uttered it before the soldiers, before these sailors and peasants and day-labourers and workers whom he regarded as the people, he felt as if he were holding to a light a mirror which magnified it. How he had once striven for newer and more meaningful words when he still gave clever lectures for young workers, and how little there actually was to say. How many useless words speech contained, while the few simple ones were still denied their right, their measure and their reality. Bread was not bread as long as it was not eaten by all, and as long as its sound was accompanied by that of hunger like a body by its shadow. One made do with a few ideas, a few words, and a passion which had no names. It was hate and love at the same time. He thought he was holding it in his hand like a light with which one illuminates and with which one kindles a fire. Killing had become as familiar to him as eating and drinking. There was no other kind of hatred. Annihilate, annihilate! Only what the eye saw dead had disappeared. Only the enemy's corpse was no longer an enemy. In burnt-out churches

155

one could no longer pray. It seemed that all his powers had rallied together in this one passion like regiments on the battlefield. It embraced the ambition of his youthful days, the hatred for his mother's uncle and his superiors at the office, the envy of the children of rich homes, the yearning for the world, the foolish expectation of woman, the marvellous bliss with which one merged with her, the bitterness of his lonely hours, his innate malice, his trained intelligence, the sharpness of his eye and even his cowardice and proneness to fear. Yes, anxiety even helped him to win battles. And with that lightning-swift shrewdness by which one is favoured only in the seconds when life itself is at stake he grasped the foreign rules of military strategy. He translated into military tactics what his innate cunning had dictated to him from earliest youth. He became a master of the art of spying out the enemy. He entered the villages and towns of the adversary in many disguises. There were no bounds to the mischievous play of his fantasy, the romantic tendencies of his nature, the perilous excursions dictated by his private curiosity. There was no superior authority to control him in the confusion of this civil war, nor was the enemy well enough organized to initiate a proper campaign according to the proper rules of modern warfare. One overrates danger when one has no experience of it, thought Friedrich. In reality it is a state to which one becomes as accustomed as to a bourgeois life with regular lunch hours. One can actually speak of the commonplaceness of danger. Smiling, he heard Parthagener's old question sounding in his ears: 'Was it really necessary?' and, smiling, answered, 'Yes! It was really necessary!' One did not come defenceless, without a homeland and outlawed, into a hostile world and let things go on as they were. One did not possess intelligence to place it at the disposal of stupidity, nor eyes to lead the blind. 'I could have become a minister!' he said to Berzejev, not without a little arrogance. 'Despite everything. We prefer to hang the ministers.'

'I should have thought you were smarter,' answered Berzejev. 'You were so sensibly undecided, so agreeably aimless, so private, without obvious passion . . .'

Friedrich interrupted him. 'It is not my world, the one into which I fell by the accident of birth. I had nothing to do in it. Now I have something to do. I always lived with the feeling of having missed my time. I did not know that I was yet to experience it.'

He conducted his own war. He had a personal account to settle with the world. He had his own tactics. Berzejev called them 'anti-military.' 'They are unbourgeois,' replied Friedrich. 'Those of the bourgeois generals are wordless, and therefore spiritless. The bourgeois commander fights with the help of orders, we fight with the help of oratory.' And once again he assembled his comrades for the third time that week and once again uttered the old new words: 'Freedom' and 'New World'!

'In the Great War your officers ordered you: "Stand to attention!" We, your comrade commanders, shout the opposite at you: "Forward." Your officers ordered you to hold your tongues. We ask that you shout, "Long live the Revolution!" Your officers ordered you to obey. We entreat you to understand. There they told you: "Die for the Tsar!" And we say to you, "Live! But if you have to die, then die for yourselves!"'

Jubilation arose. 'Long live the Revolution!' cried the crowd. And Berzejev whispered shyly: 'You are a demagogue.'

'I believe every word I say,' retorted Friedrich.

157

As soon as they marched into a captured place, he had the arrested bourgeois brought before him. They stood in a line, he studied their faces. A quiet illusion took possession of him. He found resemblances between these strangers and the faces of bourgeois acquaintances. He hated the whole class, as one hates a particular kind of animal. One looked like the writer he had met at Hilde's, another like Dr Süsskind, who tended to turn up over and over again, a third like the Prussian colonel, a fourth like the Social Democrat party leader. He let them all go again. Once there fell into his hands a harmless bank director whose face seemed familiar. But he could not remember exactly. 'What's your name?' he asked. 'Kargan,' whispered the man. 'Are you a brother of the Trieste Kargan?' 'A cousin!' 'When you write to him,' said Friedrich, 'give him my regards.' The man feared a trap. 'I never write to him,' he said. 'How large is your fortune?' asked Friedrich. 'All lost!' stammered the man. 'I had a flourishing business,' he went on. 'Fifty employees in the bank! And a small factory!' 'In feudal times,' said Friedrich to Berzejev, 'a man who ruled over fifty employees was a man. That one there's a slug, the cousin of my mother's uncle.' He noted how the large tears ran down the director's cheeks.

Once, in the street, he encountered a man who still retained a few remnants of a former elegance. Friedrich stopped. 'Come on, let him go!' said Berzejev. 'I can't,' said Friedrich, 'I must recall whom he looks like.' The man began to run. They pursued him, held him fast. Friedrich scrutinized him closely. 'Now I know!' he exclaimed, and turned the stranger loose. 'He looks like the operetta composer, L. Do you recall the photograph in the illustrated magazines? He has the same waltzing expression.' And satisfied, he began to sing: 'There are things one must forget, they are too beautiful to be true . . . .'

Of course, he did not know that he himself was gradually beginning to become a feature of the illustrated and non-illustrated newspapers of the bourgeois world, the greater part of which was not nearly annihilated. He did not know that the correspondents of ten great powers telegraphed his name whenever they had nothing else to report and that he was seized on by the mighty machinery of public opinion, that mechanism which manufactures sensations, the raw material of world history. He read no newspapers. He did not know that every third day he featured in the series of men who formed a constant column in the press under the title 'The bloody executioners', alongside the columns about boxers, composers of operettas, long-distance runners, child prodigies and aviators. He underrated – like all the more judicious of his comrades – the mysterious technique of the defence mechanism of society, which lay in making the extra-ordinary ordinary by exaggeration or by going into detail, and by letting it be established through a thousand 'well-informed sources' that the riddles of history consisted of real events. He did not know that this world had grown too old for ecstasy, and that technique could master the material of legend to transform eternal verities into current affairs. He forgot that there were gramophones to reproduce the thunders of history, and that the cinema could recall blood-baths as well as horse-races.

He was naïve, for he was a revolutionary.

2

Thanks to the extraordinary length of time the war had taken to run its course, many letters had stayed so long in the post that they did not reach their destination for years. The letter that Friedrich had written to Hilde in the winter of 1915 was received by her in the spring of 1919, at a time when she had long ceased to be Fräulein Hilde von Maerker and was now the wife of Herr Leopold Derschatta, or von Derschatta, which he was no longer entitled to call himself after the Austrian revolution. Nevertheless, he was called Herr Generaldirektor since no one is willingly deprived of his rank in the Middle European countries, and since one feels just as respected for the title that may be spoken by others as for that which one bears oneself.

Herr von Derschatta had in fact been a Director General during the last two years of the war, having been sent back from the field as a lieutenant in the reserve, with a minor gunshot wound of the elbow which he had quite unnecessarily exposed to the enemy above the parapet. His enemies – for a Director General always has enemies – maintained that he knew what he was doing. But let us pay no attention to his enemies! Their calumnies are unimportant. Even if we assume that the gunshot wound had been no accident, what help was a gunshot wound to anyone? How many did a gunshot wound save from returning to the field? No, Herr von Derschatta, who had become a railway station commandant like Hilde's father at the outbreak of war, although he should not have remained behind the front at his age, and who only went into the field as the result of an oversight for which a major at the War Office later had to make amends – this Herr von Derschatta needed no gunshot wound. He had protection. His family, who came from Moravia, had produced government officials for generations, ministerial advisers, officers, and only one single Derschatta had shown talent and become an actor – and he bore another name. Connections with one of the oldest families in the land originated with great-grandfather Derschatta, who had been a simple steward of a count's estates. What a piece of luck for the great-grandson! For the descendant of that count was now a powerful man in the government and whoever called himself his friend did not have to dread the war. When Herr von Derschatta left hospital with his arm finally healed, he had resolved not to visit the front again. He betook himself, his arm still in the black bandage for appearance's sake, to the office where his friend ruled. He strode without stopping – as if he represented his own fate – though long, empty and echoing passages and other narrow corridors in which whole swarms of civilian rabble waited for passports, permits and identification papers, he saluted lackadaisically whenever an usher jumped to his feet who – thanks to a vocational capacity for presentiment – immediately divined that here there wandered a lieutenant with connections, and, after some enquiries, reached his friend's door. He remained in friendly conversation for exactly ten minutes : 'Excellency,' he said, 'may I be permitted . . . .'

'I know already,' Excellency replied, 'I received the letter from Herr Papa. What's new? What's Fini up to?'

'Your Excellency is very kind,' said Herr von Derschatta.

'As always, as always!' opined His Excellency. 'A splendid young woman!'

And as the lieutenant rose, the Count, as if by chance, as if he were thinking aloud about something that had nothing at all to do with his guest, let fall the words: 'All settled tomorrow.'

Thereby the Count meant nothing other than the Potato Board, whose task it was to check free enterprise in potatoes and to prevent profiteering. The Potato Board at that time was still run by an expert, one of the richest farmers, who, despite his fitness for service in the field, had already been thrice designated as indispensable and who, unluckily for him, had not looked up his protector in the Food Ministry for six months. Out of sight, out of mind! When the military had recently claimed the greengrocer, he was – to the surprise even of the military – no longer regarded as indispensable. It was Herr von Derschatta who had become indispensable instead. And with the manifest reason that in such serious times a Potato Board must be subordinate to the War Minister no less than to the Minister for Food, the lieutenant, as a member of the Army, was allocated to establish a lasting liaison between the War Minister and the fruit of the earth.

From now on Herr von Derschatta called himself Director General, although it was not expressly made known that this was his title. Could one possibly have called him Lieutenant in such serious times, when every other lawyer was a lieutenant? Someone, some day uttered the title Director General Derschatta, and from then on he was known as Director General Derschatta. Indeed, some weeks later there reappeared that farmer who had once reigned as indispensable. But in what a pitiable state! He had had to drill for four weeks, that is, until his family had found satisfactory protection. He was finally restored to his potatoes, no longer as sovereign but as Derschatta's technical adviser, and had to content himself with the title of Director.

Derschatta, who was by nature a prudent man, did not enjoy seeing the farmer in his vicinity. Two men fit for war service in proximity did not go down well. Besides, he badly needed a secretary and equally feared to deprive the trenches of three men. He therefore began by attempting to dislodge the farmer. But the latter sat fast. Thereupon he relinquished his claim to a male secretary and decided to remain on the lookout for a female substitute.

Hilde, who had long since tired of being a sick-nurse, and who considered that employment with the Red Cross was more a tribute to her benevolence than fitting for her intellect, had for some months been seeking a post in the public service, one – as it were – as the right hand of an important man. Frau G., her friend, who knew Herr Derschatta, brought Hilde to his notice. Herr von Derschatta treasured womanly charm. And as, in those serious times, it was no longer unusual for daughters from good homes to sit at typewriters, thus serving the Fatherland as well as emancipation, Hilde rapidly learned to type and became a lady secretary.

She was proud, according to the usage of her times, thereby to 'earn her bread'. Her father had grown tired, worn down by the admonitions of his housekeeper, whom he had still not yet married, and by the opposition of his daughter; he was already weary of his post at the railway station, the war was going on too long for his liking, he longed for his quiet office again, the peaceful clubroom, a crisp poppy-seed croissant, his stomach was so upset by the maize flour and, in a word, he allowed his daughter to become a secretary without opposition.

He would not have done so, despite his tiredness, if he had been more closely acquainted with Herr von Derschatta – and also, of course, with his daughter. For Hilde, who was as convinced of the absurdity of the old morality as she was of her own self-sufficiency, was enraptured by the discovery made by girls of the middle class during the war – that a woman could dispose of her body as she wished, and, if only to comply with theory, offered no resistance at all to the demands made by Herr Derschatta on his secretary. It was an era in which women, while they were abused, were motivated by the concept that they were obliged to do something by which they differed from their mothers. While the conservatives bemoaned the notorious laxity of morals, virginity was remarked on by the men as a rare phenomenon and regarded by the flappers as an encumbrance. Many women derived no pleasure at all because they practised sexual intercourse as an obligation, and because their pride in venturing to love like men satisfied them more than love itself. Herr von Derschatta did not need to feign love. Hilde's ambition to be able to assess men only by their physical prowess, in the same way as men formed their opinions of women, made any exertions on Derschatta's part unnecessary from the outset as far as she was concerned. Without a trace of passion or pleasure, simply on grounds of principle, Hilde had relations with the Director General, naturally in office hours, because she could then at the same time retain the awareness of being the 'right hand' of an important functionary. If anything really attracted her in this adventure, it was curiosity. But even in the curiosity there was mingled a kind of investigating scientific zeal. And the love hours passed like the office hours, from which they were in a sense subtracted, in a cool concupiscence that felt like the brown leather of the office sofa on which they were consummated. Meanwhile the yellow pencil and typist's notebook lay on the carpet awaiting further employment, for the Director General did not like to waste time and began to dictate even while he was engaged in satisfying the requirements of hygiene at the tap. It was, one might say, a love idyll on the Pitman system and corresponded completely to the seriousness of the times and the danger that beset the Fatherland.

It would certainly have remained without consequence if it had not become involved with the fate of a clerk named Wawrka. Wawrka had been indispensable until Derschatta's arrival and had grown accustomed to regarding war as an event that did not endanger his life. But the Director General, who, in that very context, was disposed to have as few healthy men around him as possible, annulled Wawrka's indispensability. The latter, in a long audience, implored the Director General for clemency. The poor man fell on his knees before the great Derschatta. He invoked his numerous family, his six children – he had invented two more for the emergency – his sick wife, who of course was really perfectly well. But the Director General's concern for his own life rendered him even more unyielding than he was by nature; it was settled : Wawrka had to join up.

The poor man resolved on revenge. He knew who Hilde's father was and, with his simple brain, which did not appreciate the philosophy of an emancipated young woman, assumed that the goings-on on the sofa which he had overheard must be the result of a seduction in the good old style. With persons of consequence, he thought in his innocence, there is an honour which one forfeits, protects, avenges in a duel or with pistol-shots. He already saw the Director General lying dead in the office with a bullet in the temple, old Herr von Maerker beside him, broken but proud and silent, and – most important of all – he himself again indispensable and preserved. And he went to Herr von Maerker and related to him what he had detected and overheard. Basically, Herr von Maerker's views did not differ from those of Wawrka. The precepts of social honour required a ministerial adviser and cavalry officer to call his daughter's seducer to account. And with the matter-of-course attitude of a man who has no misgivings about his daughter but the traditions of an old chivalry in his blood, Herr von Maerker betook himself, horsewhip in hand, to the Director General.

Herr von Derschatta was determined not to die at any price, either at the front or behind the lines. To save his life he played the confessed sinner, but also the anguished lover, and begged Herr von Maerker for his daughter's hand. Hilde would have preferred to pursue her sexual freedom but realized that she must avert a catastrophe. She made a sacrifice to prejudice, got married, and consoled herself with the prospect of a free modern marriage in which both parties could do as they wished.

But she was wrong. For her husband, who had formerly shared her views of sexual freedom for women, suddenly regarded marriage as a sacred institution and was determined, as he said, to preserve 'the honour of his home'. Yes, he even became jealous. He kept his wife under surveillance. He engaged a new secretary and pursued his normal practices with her. Wawrka went to the front and had probably fallen in the meantime. Hilde, however, got a child. It was simply a precautionary measure on her husband's part. She took it as a sign of her humiliation. Thus, with Nature's help, he had demonstrated to her that it was a wife's lot to be unfree and a vessel for posterity. She hated the child, a boy, who resembled his father with malice aforethought. Now she was surrounded by two Derschattas. When the one went to the office, the other screamed in the cradle. Often they both slept in her bed. She had nobody in the world. She could not talk to her father, he did not understand what she said. Her only friend, Frau G., gave her cheap advice. She should betray her husband. That was the sole revenge. But Herr von Derschatta was mistrustful and prudent and a domestic tyrant of the old style. And far and wide there was no man with whom it would have been worthwhile breaking the marriage. For Hilde had become more critical. Misfortune makes one choosy.

Then came the Revolution. Herr von Derschatta lost his connections, his rank and his nobility. He had never had a vocation. It was necessary to cut down. The children's nurse was dismissed and a cheap cook engaged. One gave no social evenings and went to no parties. Herr von Derschatta lost his secretaries and concentrated his entire manliness on his wife. He became even more jealous. A second child arrived, a son, just as much like his father as the first and just as much hated by Hilde. Herr von Derschatta plunged into commerce. He developed connections with members of the odious but clever race of Jewish financiers. At the instance of one of these he removed to Berlin, in order to act for his principal on the money markets of German cities. No one had any confidence in his expertise. But, in the opinion of rich but ill-favoured men, he had a distinguished appearance and 'cut a good figure' in Germany. No drop of Jewish blood could be detected in him. And he was a nobleman.

He made his living by tenuous deals, which he barely grasped. He consorted with stout individuals whom he despised and whom he simultaneously respected and feared. He attempted to learn their 'dodges'. For he believed they were dodges. He did not realize that generations of ancestors subjected to pogroms and martyrdom, confined in the ghetto and compelled to banking transactions, were requisite to making deals. He became one of those furtive antisemites who begin to hate out of respect and who say to themselves a thousand times a day, whenever a deal goes against them and whenever they believe themselves outwitted : 'If I were to have my life over again, I would be a Jew.' A great part of his bad humour arose from the fact that it was so difficult to be born again. And because he could not discuss his private worries with business friends and acquaintances, he poured out his heart to Hilde. She let him talk, she did not comfort him, she actually rejoiced in his bad luck. She was haughty and spiteful. The Director General who, with the adroitness of a weakling, approved the principles of the new world and despised those of the old one, which was what he called a 'reorientation', indicated that his marriage had been an over-hasty affair and the result of a reactionary outlook. He thought of his marriage as he did of his patriotism and his war decoration and his monarchistic opinions. From the whole of that world, which had so rapidly collapsed, he had salvaged nothing but this stupid marriage, whose basis had been a stupid principle of honour. Today? Today no reasonable man would enter into a discussion with an old blockhead of a ministerial adviser over the honour of his daughter.

Pistols, horsewhips, duels, formalities! What a performance! 'If I had not married Hilde,' he thought bitterly, 'I might now have got hold of the daughter of a rich Jew. Blond Aryans are highly sought after.' Often he worked himself into a rage. He no longer had a uniform or a title or any position of standing. No precepts anywhere could force him to practise restraint. He let himself go. A door slammed, a chair fell over, his fist pounded on the table, the hanging-lamp began to shake gently. Hilde opened her eyes wide. Already grief choked her, the tears began to smart at the corners of her eyes. 'Anything rather than cry,' she thought, 'anything rather than cry in front of him! I shall try instead to be surprised, just surprised. What an animal. A butcher.' First the nape of his neck reddened, then the blood mounted from behind into his face. Small hairs sprouted on the backs of his broad hands. She must think of someone quickly, thought was a comfort in itself. And she thought of her father, who restrained himself a hundred times a day, who was doubly polite when he fell into a silent rage, who left the house when he had something unpleasant to say. Father! But he was old and foolish and had never understood her. Even if he were here now, he would at most shoot it out with her husband.

She remembered Friedrich. She no longer saw him distinctly. She remembered him, but not as a living human being, rather as a kind of 'interesting phenomenon'. A young idealist, a revolutionary. And not even consistent. In the end he was like the others. 'He must have enlisted and has probably been killed,' she thought.

She had not ceased thinking of Friedrich when the Director General succeeded, the inflation overcome, in obtaining an impressive and prominent position as

169

manager of the office of a steel combine in Berlin, and in acquiring the improved mood that befitted the circumstances.

One day the maid brought her a letter. The envelope was studded with many postmarks. The comments of many postal officials criss-crossed at the edges. The round postmarks lay like medals on someone's chest. The letter was like a warrior who had emerged from a heated engagement. It bore her old address, her maiden name, for which she yearned, and she regarded the letter with that tenderness with which she so often recalled her girlhood days. It was, in any case, a delightful letter. It had sought her out after long endeavour and fruitless journeys, it was a loyal devoted letter. 'It comes from one who is long dead,' she thought, and redoubled her tenderness at this notion. She carefully cut it open. It was Friedrich's last letter.

From the first word he was at once close to her. She recalled his gait, his greeting, his gestures, his voice, his silence, his hand. His face she no longer saw distinctly. She felt his timid touch on her arm, she smelled the scent of the evening rain through which they had walked together, and saw the twilight in the little café. A sudden pang checked her recollections. He was dead. He had perished in the confusion of the times. Dead in some prison, starved, executed. 'I should go into mourning,' she thought, 'put on mourning. He was the only real man I ever met. And look how I treated him!'

But when her husband entered the room her mourning had disappeared or had been relegated to the background, or overlaid with a bright triumph. The Director General was puzzled by his wife's good humour. She irritated him, he did not know why. What reason could she have for being so cheerful? 'I've had enough irritations already today. I'll spoil her mood.' And aloud : 'Why are you so exuberant?' She looked at him and did not reply. She did not feel the choking pain and she was sure that she would not cry. The letter lay in the drawer and radiated secret strength. Derschatta's sons came in from their daily outing. They had healthy red empty faces and squabbled eternally. She sent the children away with the maid. She ate nothing. For the first time she noticed exactly how her husband behaved at table. He must have learned as a child how to hold a knife and fork and yet he ate like a savage. His gaze wandered over the narrow columns of the unfolded newspaper and his spoon rose gropingly, like a blind man, to his mouth. Although he seemed preoccupied with some item of news, this in no way lessened his comfortable enjoyment in eating. 'What an appetite!' thought Hilde, as if appetite were a degrading quality. 'How remarkably some people behave.' She felt as if her husband were a stranger, whom she had met in a restaurant. He was no concern of hers. She was free.

How could she set about discovering something about Friedrich's fate? If she were bolder, she could go out into the world, travel to Russia to seek him out. She discarded this romantic idea. Yet it seemed to her that nothing one felt was fanciful when one loved. What could be more remarkable than what she had experienced already? Their first encounters, his departure, his imprisonment in Siberia, his return, his disappearance, and finally this letter! Did it not come to her as if guided from heaven? Was it perhaps a cry for help, which she heard too late? It was all miraculous, there was no doubt, and it was not for her to flinch from an improbable task.

3

When he stood at the lectern and addressed the young people, the burden of his experiences oppressed him and he felt old, as if he were a hundred. Often, at home, he looked in the mirror and persuaded himself that his face was no older than ten years ago. The youth and health of the others, however, seemed to be a reflection of attitudes rather than physical characteristics. They were six, eight or ten years younger than he. They understood what he told them with ease. And yet, with each sentence he thought: 'I'm serving as a textbook of history here, and not even an orthodox one.' Often a small word betrayed the former rebel in him. Then he would feel a shudder passing rapidly over the backs of his listeners. He paused. He felt as if he must suddenly stop short, from lack of words. Passion had been taken by surprise. None of these young men had walked, lonely and hostile, through the streets of cities as he had. Singing and carrying flags, they marched to fêtes, lectures and meetings. Like conquerors, they entered into the inheritance of a new world, but they had conquered nothing and they were only heirs. They no longer needed to answer hatred with hatred. Not one of them need be homeless and wretched any longer. Sorrow was banned, a reactionary institution. A new race was to arise, it was already here, with happy muscles, sunny eyes, fearless because there were no terrors now and brave because no dangers threatened. He had not grown old, it was just that the world had become new, as if he had lived a thousand years. And he learned to experience the slow indifference of the elderly, which gradually spreads over their bodies and soon covers the living like a shroud. The pains came like muffled noises, the pleasures kept a respectful distance, delights he already experienced in the past even as he tasted them, like their own traces left behind years ago. They were recollections of delights.

It was probably the same for the others, his comrades and contemporaries, but they immersed themselves in work. They sat at the desks which had replaced the throne as the furniture of those in government. They wrote and read and avoided the streets. Their windows looked out over the distant outskirts of the city or into the courtyards of the Kremlin. They saw either the mist of the fields, mingled with the smoke of a few factory chimneys, or a plot of grass, a few Red Army sentinels and an occasional official visitor. They travelled through the towns in closed cars. Health and disease, mortality and birth rate, hunger and satiety, crime and passion, homelessness and drunkenness, illiteracy and schools, backwardness and genius, all figured in the reports, and even what was described as the 'popular morale' acquired the physiognomy of a statistic. And everyone prophesied good things to come. Optimism became the prime duty. With their old tired faces, their sick bodies, their shortsighted, much-afflicted eyes, the old endeavoured to copy the cheerful speech and athletic sprightliness of the young, and they resembled fathers who had been taken on excursions by their sons.

'People are altogether changed,' said Friedrich to Berzejev.

'Do you still remember R.? Even he has become an optimist. He abandons his books and goes down to the soldiers for an hour. "What splendid fellows!" he says then. They treat him like a raw egg and allow him to pat them on the back. He, who once said that he feared the *canaille,* and that I ought to fear them too, is as happy as a child. The ordinary people have a sound instinct, they know what suits R. And so they do him a favour and say something offensive to him. He is delighted. He collects these mock-familiarities as a courtier did the gracious remarks of majesty in times gone by. And the soldiers oblige him by acting "The Sovereign People". Then he returns happily to his books and is convinced that he is no different from the masses. He has evidence of it. They have spoken to him frankly. He has slapped their massive shoulders with his soft fingers and they have told him openly that they have no confidence in his style of government. The people have taken to play-acting splendidly.'

'If the simple understanding I learned at my military academy qualifies me at all to understand what actually makes a bourgeois,' said Berzejev, 'I would say that our comrades have become bourgeois. Probably they always were. It was only the tension and hostility and the poverty in which they lived that inhibited their bourgeois instincts. Now the tension is over. I consider that the characteristic feature of the bourgeois is optimism. Everything will be alright. We shall soon conquer. The general knows what to do. The enemy is done for. My wife's as true as gold. Things are improving, and so on. Now they have flats with furniture and water-closets, and the children play in the corridors and get on at school. Have you seen how Savelli has installed himself? Oh, not extravagantly! It's not what the newspapers of the bourgois countries throw in our teeth. Alas, our comrades despise luxury. But they have a passionate inclination towards bourgeois comfort and knick-knacks. They say that Savelli has become very ferocious. He is responsible for eighty per cent of the executions. I was with him a week ago. He had bought himself floral teacups. He doesn't drink tea out of a glass any more. Someone has brought him a marvellous machine from Germany for making real Turkish coffee. He explained to me for a quarter of an hour how it's made and said, full of amazement, "The Germans are really brilliant fellows!" An American journalist went to visit him. He treated the American very well, that is very badly, in a superior manner. Often he replied to some question of the American's with: "That's no concern of yours!" or "Tell your boss that we treat bourgeois journalists much more kindly than they deserve." But when the American had left, Savelli said after a few minutes' reflection: "A fine nation, these Americans. They know exactly what they want." Just wait two years, and Savelli will tell the Americans as much to their face.'

'In the whole of Russia,' said Friedrich, 'how many are there still who talk as we do? The people who fought with us have disappeared, have gone home, are townsfolk and workers and clerks again. How few have remained with us! They're starting to reorganize the army. People already treat our kind with respect. A comrade gave me his seat on the tram. I'm getting old, we're all getting old.'

A week later R. said to Friedrich:

'It would probably be best for you not to stay in Moscow with your pessimism. One of our people has suggested that you should go to the Volga district.'

'Don't lie to me!' exclaimed Friedrich. 'Admit that it's you who suggested it.'

'Alright then, *I* suggested it! I wanted to spare you any awkwardness.'

'Nobody asked you to. I shall stay here as long as I like.'

'You won't succeed,' said R. 'You'll go, voluntarily or involuntarily, Savelli will see to that. Besides, have you read my article? I have written an attack on pessimism. Naturally, I mean you and your lot.'

'Do you recall,' said Friedrich, 'what you told me about Savelli in Vienna? You thought that he would hang us!'

'I was talking about a different Savelli. There *is* a difference. Savelli was powerless. And today – he no longer even uses his old name – he is no longer powerless.'

'And you are telling me this because you're afraid?'

'Not afraid. Out of caution. And conviction. Savelli must not know of our discussion. What's more, I warn you not to mention it to anyone at all.'

'Speak plainly! You're saying that you've taken it on yourself to get me out of the way, gently. You're saying that you're all afraid I might be ambitious. I'm not, any more. I don't care a damn for your Revolution.'

'So much the better. Then get away quickly. But don't tell anyone. I shall never admit that I've spoken to you.'

'But *I* heard your discussion,' suddenly exclaimed Berzejev. He had opened the door, so that they could see the corridor.

'I've been standing here for half an hour listening to you.'

He approached R. and raised his hand. R. ducked. Berzejev's blow struck his ear. The next moment he sat under the table and cried: 'Either calm down or go away!'

They went away.

'I shall probably go to Germany,' said Friedrich. 'You'll come with me, of course?'

'No!' said Berzejev. 'We shall separate. You mustn't be angry. I have to tell you frankly that I can't leave Russia. I am happy to be able to live here in safety. Safely for the first time since my youth and with nothing to hide. This is my country. I love it. I was homesick when I was abroad. I can't live abroad again. In a word – I'm staying.'

'If I were in your place,' said Friedrich slowly, 'I should feel compelled to accompany my friend.' I have no country, he thought quietly. He was too abashed to formulate it. But Berzejev guessed. 'I'm only a Russian,' he said – and it sounded like a reproach. 'I've learned nothing. I can only remain in the army. What could I do abroad? I'd only be a nuisance to you . . . .' 'Farewell!' said Friedrich. He gave him his hand, they embraced each other – lingeringly, as if each still had something to say to the other, something that could no longer be uttered. As if, still embracing, they were separated by an immense space, as if they stood on opposite shores of a lake, looked at each other, and realized that they could not catch each other's words and that there was no point in articulating them.

And three days later Friedrich again stood alone in a great station and awaited a train to the West.

It was already dusk. Soldiers who had been ordered to the frontier were sitting in the carriage. They were discussing politics.

'In Germany,' said one, 'it'll only take a week before the Revolution breaks out. Then it will happen in France, then in England, and last of all in America.'

'Blockhead,' said the other. 'Who told you that?'

'I was at a lecture that R. gave to the students.'

'What nonsense,' said the other. 'First, you didn't

understand the lecture, second, it probably had a special meaning, and third, R. is a Jew and I no longer believe a word he says. A few days ago, when I was on duty at T., he spoke to us.'

'Jew or not, we're finished with all that, there's no religion any more.'

'But there are still blockheads, since you're still alive,' cried a third and they all roared.

'Who are the clever ones, then?' asked Friedrich. They mentioned three names which echoed through Russia and the world. Finally, one mentioned the name that Savelli had now adopted. Several agreed with him.

'A splendid man,' he said. 'He knows what has to be done. I came across him once in a corridor in the X-department. The corridor was narrow and dark, I stepped back to let him pass, I greeted him, he raised his head, did not reply, only looked at me with his eyes made of night and ice. I felt cold all over. He knows what he wants. Most of the clever Jews only speak prophecies, and that is on account of the radio, just because the ignorant peasants in the villages all listen. And so one never hears anything clever any more, it's all kept for the radio.'

'Yes,' exclaimed another, 'I often think that the comrades take us for stupider than we are. They say something quite simple a hundred times. I know it by heart already. In the paper they always write the same thing, too.'

'Why should I care what they say?' thought Friedrich. 'I'm beginning a new life.'

4

But he began his new life as if he had already lived it once before. He knew it. He set foot in it like an actor on the stage in a part he has already played on many evenings, in the vague hope of some untoward incident of a minor nature which, through an emergency, assumes the nature of a sensation. He even hoped for minor misfortunes, an arrest, expulsion, perhaps a jail sentence.

Anyone else in his position would have thought of a revolution. He was surprised that the war did not recommence. When he arrived at M., the mid-German town where he had spent a few rainy days during the war, he noted that it was still raining. In the large windows of the café there still hung notices asserting that Frenchmen, Englishmen, Poles and other nationalities were unwelcome on the premises. The school was of red brick and when one passed by in the morning a chorus of clear children's voices could be heard singing *Ich hatt' einen Kameraden.* In the centre stood the red-brick church. The tax office was made of red brick. The town hall was constructed of red bricks. And although all these buildings veered towards prettiness, and seemed to have been assembled as in a game by some sort of oversized children, they nevertheless betrayed a tendency to eternity, like the Pyramids. After five or six years it was still raining. The tram still shuttled to and fro. Only the conductress had returned to hearth and home. The women still wore the same hats. Where was the comrade who, in those days, had arranged his first genuine false passport? He was alive. He had become naturalized in the meantime and been made a member of parliament. And where was the party leader? He was a member of the administration in Berlin. And, although the Communist tailor was now the furious political opponent of that Social Democratic party leader, it seemed to Friedrich, because he had not witnessed events at close quarters, that both, the Communist and the party leader, were engaged in a consistent and parallel ascent like officers or government officials who attained a higher grade after a certain period of service. And although they had both attained their rank in fighting against each other, the ironic fate that is a special feature of radical politicians conferred on them a frightening resemblance. Like the Jews, who always turn to the east when they pray, the revolutionaries always turned to the right when they began to act publicly. However radical the tailor might be, it did not affect this rule. Every month he seriously expected the revolution. He should have served a prison sentence on account of an insult he had hurled at the party leader, and he had to thank his parliamentary immunity for his present freedom. Twenty years earlier the insulted one had found himself in the same situation. But both seemed to have forgotten it. 'Who knows,' thought Friedrich, 'twenty years from now my comrade will be insulted and complain. The Revolution always remained on the left; only its champions always turned to the right.' 'Last week,' related the tailor, 'two policemen had to remove me forcibly from parliament. You should have seen the goings-on! Oh, things aren't always as peaceful for us as people in Moscow sometimes make out! We are just on the verge of a railway strike. The Party is working at full stretch. We've gained five thousand members in Hamburg. Here, in M., we're strongly represented. We can count on fifty-five per cent of the factory workers. The party funds come in absolutely on time. And twice or three times a week we have our evenings.' 'What a local kind of patriotism this comrade has!' thought Friedrich. 'It's on this basis that love of the fatherland is built. He is proud of the district that has elected him. It won't take much to make him take even the reactionary parties of his constituency under his wing and consider them better than the reactionaries of other constituencies. Here I have an opportunity, no longer rare these days, to be present at the birth of a kind of local patriotism, love of constituency, *ab ovo*. He considers *his* communists the most revolutionary. And how he's changed! He now wears a Russian blouse. The last time I was here, he was still wearing an unassuming shirt without a collar. And just as the men who make a bourgeois career acquire a double chin and a paunch, so the men who are my comrades procure a revolutionary costume and a briefcase. A few years ago he still had a hat. Now he wears a sports cap. Then he still wore his hair parted, now he combs it backwards. And he himself is unaware of this. His revolutionary posture develops as insidiously as a double chin. This comrade is reliable.'

He looked up the former party leader in the diplomatic post he now held. He was living 'according to his station'. The hall looked almost like that of the illustrious Herr von Maerker. Only the party leader's study had remained the same. Modesty is a virtue. The paperknife, shaped like a cavalry sabre, still lay on the desk. A small dome bulged over the ink-well, which resembled a mosque. The forget-me-not frames still surrounded the two sons in uniform, although happily they had returned home. And the only new object was the large oil-painting of the party leader, painted by one of the leading portraitists of the Reich. What did it matter to the painter? He painted, painted without stopping. Once the Kaiser, twice the beloved general, once a radical. Art had nothing to do with politics. The painters wanted to be left alone in their studios. Art was Christmas, a holiday when all hearts beat in the same rhythm. How handsome the party leader was in the portrait, with his gaze directed to the future of the Fatherland, his right hand supported on the corner of the desk and his left toying with an iron watch-chain, which he had substituted for the gold one! No doubt about it, it was painted grey, it was made of iron. And he did not look like a party leader, but like a leader of parties. The Kaiser had known none, but he knew them all. 'We have a passionate interest in Russia,' he began. And, with the satisfaction of a man who speaks in the name of his country, he cited Bismarck, whose reminiscences he had read in all objectivity. Ah, he had always been a non-party man! The Fatherland, like painting, had nothing to do with politics. 'In Germany,' replied Friedrich, 'the so-called Left will probably only succeed in a hundred years in being unrelenting towards their opponents. They are unable to hate. They are unable to become excited. It is their most zealous endeavour, not to defeat the enemy but to understand him. Eventually they come to know him so well that they own him to be right and can no longer attack him.'

The party leader wandered off into the wide domains of world history. It was evident that he saw himself as speaking from a tribune, and that he treated a solitary listener as an entire assembly. He loved it because he did not for a moment forget that he himself was a representative while unfailingly regarding the other, too, as a representative, and he magnified the importance he was wont to ascribe to himself by also attributing great importance to his partner. In the constant hope that each of his utterances was fitted to become a winged word, he now stressed the simple phrases and commonplaces that he had recited to Friedrich years before without pretension and as if by rote, as if they were original ideas. He had evidently, and at the first glance, remained his old self. He still appeared to be wearing the same rust-brown double-breasted jacket, and his trousers still fell in wide folds over wide smooth solid boots, the like of which were no longer to be found in shoe-maker's shop-windows and consequently looked as if they had been sought for long and zealously. But the very care the man took to be humble echoed the diligence he employed to play a central part in the history of the times. And when he repeated again and again : 'If only they'd listened to me then,' or 'Of course things turned out as I prophesied,' or 'The rashness which I have always condemned,' he appeared to be convinced that his prescience justified the sturdy neglect of his dress. And when, from time to time, he spoke of his country as 'we', he believed himself to be equally discreet and blameless in his speech. And yet his 'we', his 'our', his 'us' recalled the way in which the employees of a large department store identify themselves with their firm even though they do not share their master's income.

Some time later Friedrich was to encounter the party leader at a large assembly of politicians, journalists, diplomats and industrialists, one of those ambassadorial entertainments which are termed 'a congenial gathering' in professional circles and newspaper reports. All the men had donned tails, the uniform of congeniality. They ate sandwiches over whose butter was stretched a regular lattice of anchovy strips. Each held a plate or a cup or an empty glass in his hand without knowing why, and all sought discreetly and in vain for a place where they might dispose of these implements. Crafty guests betook themselves to the vicinity of the window-ledges and removed themselves after having deposited their plate in a perilous place, with meek expressions and in the slight anxiety that it might soon fall down and shatter. They only breathed freely when they had gained the opposite corner. The majority, however, stayed riveted to their plates and were consequently unable to be vivacious. The congeniality went from strength to strength.

Friedrich ran into a number of people here whom he had known well in Zürich. He even saw Bernardin and Dr Schleicher again. They had both become diplomats and maintained their understanding. They had sealed an alliance for life, were inseparable, and promenaded silently together because they had no more to say to each other. They had talked themselves out. They knew everything about one another. Now they were united by the memory of their bartered confessions. They were peace comrades just as two men who once met in the trenches were war comrades. Each also represented his country. And as both were concerned with so-called peaceful relations between Germany and France, and as they might have been reproached with remissness for any clouding of these relations, they both cherished peace like their own careers and their ambition accorded it the value that generals accord to war. And just as professional marriage-brokers are concerned about the bliss of the parties they have brought together, because their living depends on it, so Dr Schleicher and Bernardin were similarly concerned about peace between the two countries. They trafficked in peace as they had trafficked in state secrets during the war. Their friendship was troubled only if the name of one of them was mentioned in the newspapers more often than that of the other, or if, in the group photographs of conference participants published in the illustrated magazines, the face of one was more distinctly recognizable than that of his friend. This 'congenial gathering' too was taken by a photographer for publicity purposes, to appear under the title 'A diplomatic tea-party' in the Sunday supplements. Bernardin and Dr Schleicher separated, since they took it for diplomatic subtlety not to let their association become apparent to the other nations. While they stationed themselves in the background with heroic modesty, they pressed their faces between the shoulders of the front row so as to appear on the plate nonetheless. And furtively but persistently, in their anxiety at the crucial moment when the flash blazed out, they would discard the facial expressions they had donned as advantageous, cast sidelong glances at each other, and consider which of them was standing in a better and more prominent position. The journalists, whose vocation is ever to scent out secrets, believed that the glances of the two were the equivalent of abbreviated diplomatic Notes. And every reporter who spotted this exchange of glances thought at once of the possibility of drawing attention to it in the morning paper under the magic formula of 'as rumoured in exclusive circles'.

There was only one journalist at this gathering who considered it unworthy to pay attention to glances. This was the Dr Süsskind whom Friedrich had encountered on the train years before. To be sure, Dr Süsskind did not recognize his old travelling companion. But, even if he had recognized Friedrich, it would probably not have prevented him from remarking very audibly to one of the press attachés who had become so common after the war, and who were initiating the era of democracy : 'When I was in Austria during the war, I realized at once that we should lose the war. Perhaps you remember what I wrote after the breakthrough at Gorlice?' And as the press attaché, who was not yet sufficiently versed in diplomacy to succeed in being tactful, said 'No!', Dr Süsskind went into a detailed account of his article which had revealed a prophetic pessimism. Friedrich recalled the journalist's optimism in the train. 'I once had the pleasure,' he said to Dr Süsskind, 'of meeting you.' 'I certainly don't remember it,' said the candid journalist, for whom truth came first. 'You were sitting in the train with a Prussian colonel and an Austrian major,' persisted Friedrich. 'Quite right,' said Dr Süsskind, 'but I never noticed you.' There was no point in talking to him. As if his primary concern, before embarking on a conversation, was to fathom whether Friedrich was telling the truth, he repeated once more : 'I certainly didn't notice you!' 'Yes,' said Friedrich, to jolt the other's memory, 'your wife was waiting for you at K.' 'Ah,' replied Süsskind bleakly, 'that was not my wife, that was my sister-in-law.' And that disposed of the matter.

It was in no way remarkable to encounter Dr Süsskind's stubborn matter-of-factness in the realm of this newly hatched diplomacy. The legacy of the career diplomats who had brought about the war through folly, ambition, an unthinking pleasure in the secret game, but who at least displayed the social forms as natural qualities, fell after the war to the bourgeois intellectuals – editors, men of letters, teachers and judges – men who, with an incurable love of sincerity, endeavoured to copy the traditional tricks of international politics, and who could be seen from a mile away as striving to safeguard a so-called state secret. With diplomatic passports, for which they themselves had more respect than the customs officcials, they crossed the frontiers hiding in their sealed bags lace for their wives and liqueurs for their guests, in conformity with the familiar behaviour of the lower middle class from which they sprang. Diplomatic intercourse between the representatives of the old and the new states acquired the cosy aspect of bourgeois family occasions; and it was no accident that beer, the festive drink of sturdy uprightness, became a political intoxicant. Beer evenings were the vogue. The reconciliation of the nations was achieved under the aegis of beer, just as formerly the preparation of the war had been achieved to the accompaniment of champagne. Men had become congenial. The international dominance of the bourgeoisie had only just begun.

Within this petty bourgeois diplomacy only the representatives of the sole proletarian state mastered the old diplomatic forms. A natural cunning, acquired in long struggles with the authorities, a sharp instinct for artifice and dissimulation, a spontaneous desire to deceive friend and foe, all these conferred on the representatives of the Revolution those qualities that an ancient tradition, the inherited experience of aristocratic blood and a training in courteous insincerity had conferred on the diplomats of the vanishing old world. Of all the people Friedrich now had anything to do with – and his occupation consisted in the main of having to talk to them – not a single one seemed to him capable of that kind of impassioned deliberation without which it is impossible to have an overall view of the world. All lay like soldiers in the trenches, knowing only their own section. It was war. And as each had a rank in the services, or at least a well-defined task, each took note of the uniform and insignia of the other; and if one of them were to be asked if the man he had been negotiating with every day for years were good or bad, clever or stupid, enthusiastic or half-hearted, convinced or indifferent, the questioned one would have replied: 'Mr X, about whom you enquire, only smokes cigars, is married, negotiates with me over the concession at Tomsk and is esteemed by his superiors.' And it really was as if the so-called 'human' qualities had been the characteristic features of a period of human history long past and were now only to be found on tombstones, as inscriptions for the dead. It was as if these human qualities were gradually disappearing, like goods for which there was no longer any demand, and as if they had to be replaced by others that were now much sought after. Friedrich never succeeded in obtaining any other answer to his question as to who this or that person might be than: 'X. has left the Party, B. is editor of the Democratic newspaper, Y. is Director General of the Z. works.' And one obtained such answers, not so much because no one cared about anyone else, but because, in fact, an editor seemed to be nothing but an editor and a Director General only a Director General. One of the most intimate peculiarities that could be imparted about a man was that he practised this or that vocation, displayed this or that political opinion. And Friedrich, who had never known a vocation, thought: 'I am the only one with human qualities. I am malicious, nasty, egoistic, hard-hearted and intelligent. But no longer ambitious. My ambition is extinct. For its aim was to exercise power over human beings, not over Director Generals, editors and party members or those

188

without party. It would have been my passion to see through cunning, chastise evil, buttress justice, annihilate the vicious. I would have identified with a cause. Nothing remains for me now but to look on. For twenty years I looked on, in order to learn. For a single year I fought. I shall remain an onlooker for the rest of my life. "Was it really necessary?" said old Parthagener.'

He retained enough curiosity to engage in experiences. But it was no longer the primal curiosity, which would have wanted to know what was happening, but a sort of second-class curiosity, which sought only for confirmation of what it had already accurately surmised. Once, when Friedrich had to negotiate with the executive of an aviation company, he said to himself: 'He will be a big broad-boned man in a new light-grey suit, with hair cut short and parted on the left, a wedding-ring on his finger, no other jewellery. On his desk stands a photograph of his wife. The telephone will ring every five minutes to intimidate me. The best quality cigars and cigarettes are shut away in the drawer, so-called "smoking material" for guests lies on the table. The functional nature of the office furnishings does not exclude a certain cool leathery comfort. On the arms of soft light-yellow armchairs, squat yellow shiny ashtrays rubbed over with metal polish. The man is conservative, a moderate monarchist. He acts the honest businessman with principles, but readily lets it be recognized that he is not stupid.'

When Friedrich entered he found his conjectures confirmed. The discussion bored him from the first moment. He could have supplied an exact report of it without having taken part. To make a change and to disconcert the executive he suddenly said: 'Would you disconnect your telephone while we're talking!' The great man immediately obeyed. He pressed a button with his foot; his desk was equipped with the latest technical devices and pedals like a piano. Underneath, as if by magic, all the electrical controls came out of the floor. One saw no flex leading to the lamp or the telephone, no bell on the table, no locks on the drawers, the inkwell rested in a depression in the desk and, without the executive having to make the slightest movement, he summoned his secretary by an act of simple lightning-quick volition. Friedrich noticed how the wall suddenly opened and the secretary appeared, as if he had all along been lodged in a cleft between the bricks. 'Would you just disconnect the circuit?' said the executive, and the secretary disappeared in a trice and the wall was whole again. 'We are not as electrified as that in Russia yet!' said Friedrich, pointing to the mysterious wall. 'That I can believe!' answered the executive. 'We are far ahead in Germany.' And like a man who, out of pride at the beauty of his country, shows a foreigner the landscape and tells him the names of the mountains, valleys and rivers, the executive began to explain to Friedrich the technical secrets of his office. He said 'our' with the same emphasis with which the party leaders spoke of their party and the Fatherland. 'Our installation,' he said, 'was completed only three months ago. All the wiring is in the floor, under the carpet. Here, under the desk, you see three buttons that light up red, green and yellow. The red is an alarm signal, the green is my secretary, and the yellow my lady secretary. If I press the wall here, the picture springs out.' He pressed, and the portrait, which showed the head of the firm, flew out of its frame like a window pushed open by a gust of wind, and revealed a secret compartment containing banknotes and documents. 'I need only draw this curtain,' continued the executive, 'and I am in the midst of my family circle.' The curtain opened and Friedrich saw a niche with life-sized coloured pictures showing a woman and two boys in sailor-suits. In the ceiling above the pictures a small lamp burned, so that the niche appeared like an altar. He drew nearer and recognized Hilde's portrait. It had been painted by the painter with the bushy eyebrows. He immediately resolved to find out where the Director General lived, just in case and not in order to disturb family life. 'Your wife,' Friedrich ventured to say, 'is very beautiful.' 'We have been married ten years,' replied the executive confidingly, 'but we are no longer deeply in love!' And he glanced at a shiny steel ruler as if the word 'deeply' were a term for a specific measure of love. He stood up again and seemed to reflect. He returned to the smooth wall, touched a yellow flower on the wallpaper, and immediately a small door sprang open and revealed the gilt back of a thick leather volume. This back also opened and now Friedrich perceived that it was not a book, but a small cupboard for glasses and liqueur bottles. 'One can't talk properly without a drink!' said the executive. After one glass, he became loud and exuberant, slapped Friedrich a few times on the knee and made one of the secret drawers in the green desk fly open, revealing to Friedrich pornographic postcards and hygienic objects of an erotic nature. 'Dear friend,' said the executive, 'the sexual department. Sexuality is an important factor.' And he began to spread out his pictures.

He collected them together and became serious again. 'Distractions are necessary,' he said. 'I work ten, twelve, fourteen hours a day.' And he raised his arm high and made a few gymnastic movements reminiscent of those music-hall acrobats who give their muscles a work-out before their act, as an indication that the weights they are about to lift are really heavy.

'The executive Herr von Derschatta,' Friedrich wrote subsequently in his report, 'is a good-natured man. His income is large, his family life peaceful, his industry boundless. He is incorruptible. He loves his country, for it is a branch of his firm. The conditions I set out below do not seem to me to be the last word. It would be easier to deal with him if one intimidated him. He is servile by preference.'

Friedrich wrote such reports with great care, although he knew that they had a long and devious route ahead of them and that they availed little. Even as he folded them up and put them in an envelope, he saw the many stages of the journey they had to make and the faces of the men who would be dealing with them. He knew personally some of the members of the new bureaucracy which had spread over the entire country like flocks of crows, left behind by war and revolution. He recalled their subordinate faces, on which the inflexibility of a rigid outlook conferred the traits of a cruel piety. A small envy determined their brave words and their hesitant deeds, a minute and narrow envy, the brother of an early disillusioned ambition. Friedrich recalled how all of them – photographers and minor authors, shady lawyers and small accountants, book-keepers and nervous tradesmen – had dashed for the empty office-stools about which the soldiers of the Revolution did not concern themselves. The soldiers returned to their fields, which could not yet be tilled, to the machines which were still at a halt. The others, who had written and copied manifestoes, ordinances, plans, textbooks and pamphlets during the civil war, kept the pens in their hands, the pens, the thin steel instruments, the strongest tools of power. But it so happened that the men who were at liberty to demonstrate their talents and strength possessed no talents, and only sufficient strength to shove their opposite number away from the desk with their elbows and to reappear at the desk if the other had succeeded in dislodging them. He recalled the triumph afforded him during the war by the awareness of not being a cipher like the others, and not having to disobey sealed orders that were issued somewhere behind thick oppressive walls by anonymous tools of an unknown authority. He had succeeded in cheating the register that had waited, blank and white, for his names and dates, in evading the pointed pens coloured with poisonous green ink which a hundred thousand clerks had aimed at him like lances. He could still see an official at the police station, a mixture of bull and farmhand, to whom he had handed the false registration form with a childish rage. 'Was it really necessary?' Parthagener had asked.

Now Friedrich himself wrote reports for registers. And all the acrobatics with which he had assumed and discarded names, disguised and simulated existences, had only led him to become himself a tool, an object of the offices and bureaux. Would the paperwork never cease? What kind of decree was it that conferred on the most fragile and delicate of materials – paper, pencil and pen – power over blood and iron, brains and brawn, fire and water, hunger and epidemic? Only a moment ago the thousand chancelleries had been burnt down. He himself had set fire to them. He himself had seen their crumbling ashes. And already they were writing again in a hundred thousand chancelleries, and already there were new small books with green and red lines, and already every man

had a code-number in an office as small children have a
guardian angel in heaven. 'I will not!' cried Friedrich. 'I
will not!' he thought, while he himself sat in an office
and dictated to a girl in a blue sailor's costume. How
nimbly the pen ran with her hand! It was a Koh-i-noor,
shiny yellow with a long black tip. Then the girl went into
the big general office and the machine began to clatter.
And the report found itself in the courier's briefcase. He
entered a secretariat. There sat Dr M., a small plump
man with a face which seemed to consist of nothing but
protuberances, and tiny malevolent eyes under a brow
full of meaningless furrows, the consequences of a mood
of the skin and not of careful thought. He hated Friedrich. He wanted to be abroad writing reports himself.
Just as the front-rank party chiefs did not desire to go
abroad, but endeavoured to remain in Moscow at any
price, so the mediocre subordinates desired nothing more
ardently than a sojourn in a bourgeois foreign country
where they could live out their bourgeois tendencies.
They wanted to drink good beer, to sit at a well-laid table.
Was that not what one meant by the cause of the proletariat?

But what was the cause of the proletariat? These
deputies, who let themselves be imprisoned and were set
free again, these anonymous proletarians who were forgotten in the penitentiaries, the shot and the hanged, what
use were they? How did it come about that the very ones
who were attempting to construct a new world behaved
according to the oldest superstition, the oldest, most ab-
surd superstition of the profit and sanctity of sacrifice?
Was it not the Fatherland that demanded sacrifice? Was
it not religion that demanded sacrifice? Alas, the Revolution too demanded it! And it drove men to the altars,

and everyone who submitted himself to sacrifice died in the conviction that he died for something great. And meanwhile it was the living who came off best! The world had grown old, blood was a familiar sight, death a trivial matter. All died to no purpose and were forgotten a year later. Only romanticism, like paper, was immortal.

'I serve without belief,' Friedrich told himself. 'Twenty years ago it would have been called villainy. I draw my salary without convictions. I despise the men with whom I associate, I do not believe in the success of this Revolution. Between the lines of the brazen materialistic statutes that govern at least the civilized part of the world, on the other hand, there are still unknown, unreadable secrets.'

He stood there like a captain whose ship has sunk and who, contrary to duty and against his will, remains alive thanks to a malicious fate : preserved for life on earth, on an alien planet.

5

Friedrich fell ill.

He lay alone in his room, in fever's soft delirium, and cosseted by solitude for the first time. Till now he had known only its cruel constancy and its obstinate muteness. Now he recognized its gentle friendship and caught the quiet melody of its voice. No friend, no loved one and no comrade. Only thoughts came, like children, simultaneously begotten, born and grown. For the first time in his life he learned to know illness, the beneficent pressure of soft hands, the wonderful deceptive feeling of being able to get up but unwilling to rise, the capacity to lie and float suspended at the same time, the strength that comes from loneliness like grace from misfortune, and the mute colloquy with the wide grey sky that filled the window of his high-up room, the only guest from the outside world. 'When others are ill,' he thought, 'a friend comes, asks if he may smoke a cigarette, gives the patient his hand, which it then occurs to him to wash – on hygienic grounds. The sweetheart deploys her maternal instinct, proves to herself that she can love, makes a small flirtatious sacrifice, overcomes her reluctance to take hold of ugly objects with a delicate hand. The comrades come with optimistic bustle, bringing the tenor of events to the bed-side in forced witty disguise, laugh too loudly and smile indulgently and obtain an assurance of their own health, just as the charitable involuntarily feel in their own pockets to check their spare change at the sight of a beggar. Only I am alone. Berzejev has stayed in Russia. He has a fatherland. I have none. It is possible that in a hundred or two hundred years time no human being in the world will have a place they can call home or asylum. The earth will look the same everywhere, like a sea, and just as a sailor is at home wherever there is the sound of water, so everyone will be at home wherever grass grows, or rock or sand. I was born too late or too early. I am one of the experiments that Nature makes here and there before she decides to bring forth a new species. When my fever wanes I shall get up and go away. I shall literally fulfil my fate to be a stranger. I shall prolong the mild abandon-ment of the fever a little, and wandering will transform my solitude into good fortune, as the illness has almost done.'

His fever waned. He got up. Because he had known no childhood and no mother, and because he had grown up without hearing the names of diseases and discussions as to their causes, he was not even curious to know what had been wrong with him. But he had to specify a disease to obtain his leave. He allowed himself to be told what people called the condition he had suffered from. He took six months' leave. 'I am now committing what is known as a shabby trick,' he told himself. 'According to the moral attitudes of this stupid world, it is bad enough to work for a cause of which one is not as convinced as the majority of stewards of that cause. But it's even worse to break off from this sort of work and take money for it. Both bourgeois society and its revolutionary opponents have the same appropriate term for a character such as myself. They call such behaviour cynical. Cynicism is never permitted to the individual. Only countries, parties and guardians of the future may make use of it. For the individual there is nothing left but to show his true colours. I am a cynic.'

He therefore supplied himself with money and – as so many times in his life – with a passport in a false name. The Revolution had become legitimized by diplomatic subterfuge. A false passport no longer gave Friedrich any pleasure. Even a reactionary police force acknowledged the pseudonym of a revolutionary like the incognito of a Balkan prince. Only the newspapers, which were paid by fearful industrialists, sometimes thought they were giving the government of their country a piece of information when they reported that this or that dangerous emissary of the revolution had arrived under a false name. In reality, it was the government who strove to conceal the dangerous man from the newspapers. The times were past when Friedrich had conceived himself as waging a personal battle against the world order and its defenders by means of hazardous stratagems and superfluous dissembling. Now he possessed an unwritten but internationally recognized right to illegality.

And he travelled through the great cities of the civilized world. He saw the museums, in which the treasures of the past were hoarded in depositories like furniture for which one cannot find a use. He saw the theatres, on whose stages a slice of life was picked out, divided into acts, and portrayed by persons in pink make-up for an entrance fee. He read the newspapers in which reports were spread over current events like seductive veils over uninteresting objects. He sat in the cafés and the restaurants, in which people were collected like goods in a shop-window. He frequented the poor taverns where that part of society termed the 'people' diverted itself and enjoyed the vigorous robust glitter which is associated with the pleasures of poverty. As if he had never belonged to them, he visited like a stranger the halls in which they had gathered to hear about politics and to feel that they were part of the world's bustle. And, as if he himself had never addressed them, he marvelled at their naïve enthusiasm, which greeted the hollow sound of a phrase as the devotion of the pious greeted the dull clang of a cheap bell. As if there had been no Revolution and no war! Nothing! Obliterated! Young men with wide floating trousers, with padded shoulders and flirtatious soft hips, a whole generation of sexless aviators permeated every layer of society. Football strengthened the muscles of the young workers in the same measure as those of the young bankers' sons and gave the faces of both the same traits of presence of mind and absence of thought. The proletarians trained for revolution, the bourgeois for enjoyment. Flags waved, men marched, and just as particular vaudeville acts were repeated in every large town, so in every large town an Unknown Soldier lay buried. Even in the smaller places Friedrich encountered monuments to the fallen, as he did tap-dancing Negroes.

Now his eyes saw that 'life' whose distant, mysterious and wonder-revealing reflection had been shed over the wishes of his early years. It was exactly as if he had taken the play of the dark-red light, cast by an advertising sign on the window-panes opposite, for the reflection of a great and sinister conflagration. Now he saw the sources of his fine illusions. And he derided himself with the satisfaction a clever man experiences when he uncovers errors. He went around and uncovered one source after another, and he was triumphant because he won the day against himself.

In time all the sources were exposed, quicker than he had expected. Thus he learned to know forlornness in strange cities, the aimless wandering through the early twilight of evenings, when the silvery lanterns light up and afflict the body of the abandoned with the pain of a thousand sudden needle pricks. He walked through rain-soaked streets, over the gleaming asphalt of wide squares like stony lakes, coat-collar turned up, fastened from outside, and before him only his gaze to steer him through a foreign land. He rose early, walked in the bright morning full of hurrying people. Women he did not look at illuminated him with their beauty, children laughed from gardens, a forgiving clemency emanated from slow old men who seemed doubly venerable and doubly slow among the hurrying throng. Finally, there were days that revealed all the simple and indestructible beauty, days on which his wish to be able to begin life anew was almost exceeded by the solace that he could begin again without effort.

When the spring came, he found himself in Paris. Every night he walked through smooth and silent streets, encountered the fully-laden waggons on their way to the market halls, the even trot of the heavy shaggy horses, the pious rural tinkling of their bells, the shiny green of the neatly stacked bundles of cauliflowers and the smooth whiteness of their faces among the broad drooping leaves, the artificial pale red of the thin-tailed carrots, the bloody, moist and heavy glisten of the massive butchered cattle. Every night he visited a cellar where people danced, sailors, street-girls, whites and coloured men from the colonies. The accordion poured gay march tunes into the bright room, it was the instrument of exuberant melancholy. He liked it because it reminded him of his revolutionary comrades, because it was the music of abandonment and carefreeness, because it called to mind both peaceful evenings in eastern villages and the brooding heat of African deserts, because it contained both the song of the frost and the eternal stillness of summer. From every wall wide mirrors reflected the lavish rows of lamps on to the ceiling, made twenty rooms out of one, multiplied the dancing-girls a hundredfold. He no longer noticed the stairs and the door that led outside to the nocturnal streets. The mirrored walls sealed off the room more finally than stone and marble and transformed the cellar into a single endless subterranean paradise. He sat at a table and drank Schnapps. Once, in a moment when it seemed to him that he need have no fear of revealing himself because it was the last night of the world and there would be no morrow, he asked for a piece of paper and wrote, without any form of address :

'I have not thought of you for many years. For several days I have been unable to get you out of my mind. I know that you no longer think of me. You lead a life which, today as always, is as remote from mine as one planet from another. However, this gives you my address. To be candid, I must confess that it is in no way an irresistible compulsion that induces me to write to you. Perhaps it is only an irresistible hope . . . .'

He went into the street. Dawn began to break, today as ever; the world had not perished. A blue light lay over the houses, someone opened a window. A car engine growled obstinately and rebelliously. In the light of the waking day Friedrich put the letter into the post-box.

6

These were no longer momentous times. The post functioned normally. The letter reached Hilde after an interval of three days. Then, one evening, when Friedrich returned to his hotel, someone was waiting for him.

He sat for a long time in his overcoat, damp and steaming from the rain, hat in hand and silent. She told him about her husband and children, of her bitter years, of her old father. She had, incidentally, brought him with her. He intended to visit a spa. He was there to reassure her jealous husband. They were now doing well. Her husband had made good use of his mediocrity. The others, the speculators with the inborn instinct for business, had been overwhelmed by the storms they had conjured up, like warriors fallen in adventures they had themselves provoked. Herr von Derschatta, however, was one of those mediocre bureaucrats of the business world who gain much though they risk nothing. She spoke in the jargon which is the mother tongue of Director Generals, of the 'position' that permitted certain things but not yet, or no longer, permitted others. A few strangers entered the room where they were sitting. She ceased her account. But the silence that ensued was capable of expressing all the admissions and completing all the half-admissions that she had minimized and half suppressed earlier. This silence disconcerted her the more in the presence of the other people. As if they were both as young as they had once been in the café, the fortuitousness of the external situation left them at a loss. Outside it was raining. Here strangers were sitting. 'If she comes to my room now,' he thought, 'it is decided. She is expecting it.' He said nothing.

'Perhaps we should go up to your room?' After the long silence it seemed as if she had prepared herself for this question.

They walked up the stairs; the presence of a stranger in the lift, a witness of their confusion, would have embarrassed them. They walked in silence, separated by a great distance, as if they were going upstairs to settle an old score. She sat down without removing her coat. Her small hat-brim shaded her eyes. Her coat was fastened up to her chin and her gaze held something valiant, ready for battle. She still felt the resolve with which she had got into the train. Friedrich walked over to the window, a movement made by every other man embarrassed by the presence of a woman in his room. 'Why are you silent?' she said suddenly. Anxiety trembled in her question. He heard the fear and, at the same time, the first *Du* that had passed between them. It was like the first lightning in spring. He turned round, thought, 'Now she is going to cry', and saw two moist eyes that gazed straight at him, fearless because armed with tears.

He wanted to say: 'Why did you come here? He corrected himself. He considered which would be less hurtful, 'why' or 'what for', and finally settled for a harmless 'how' in conjunction with a *Du*. So he said: 'How did you get here?'

With the rapid presence of mind that women achieve when they embark on a rash adventure, she had brought her father to assuage the vigilance of the Director General. This novelettish inventiveness alarmed him. So as not to be silent any longer, he said: 'Then you're here with your father?'

'Say what you're thinking,' she began. 'Say that you never expected me, that it was only a mood, that letter. You had probably been drinking when you wrote it.'

'Yes,' he replied, 'it was a sort of deep serious mood. I did not expect you. What I say now is in sorrow, not reproach: you should have come ten years ago. Too much has happened in between.' 'Tell me,' she said.

'It's not possible straight off. I would not know where to begin. Neither would I know what was important. It occurs to me that the facts are less important than the things one can't recount. For instance, what is more serious than any battle I have taken part in is the despair I go around in, or a word someone lets fall here and there that sometimes reveals human beings to me and sometimes humanity as a whole. But it will probably suffice to tell you the name under which I have lived for the past ten years.' And he told her his pseudonym, of which he had been so proud.

As if this name, which she had heard and read without realizing whom it concealed, were conclusive evidence of her blindness and guilt, she began to cry. 'Now I ought to go and kiss her,' thought Friedrich. He noticed how, in the midst of her despair, she took off her hat and smoothed her hair, which she now wore cut short like everyone else, and he approached, glad that he had something to do, and took the hat from her hand.

She shook her head, rose, asked with her eyes for the hat, and said quietly : 'I must go.'

'I shall let her go,' he thought.

But now, when she lifted both arms to put on her hat, she seemed to him in despair, and therefore doubly beautiful, as he had never seen her before. She was young, she had let the years pass by like zephyrs, she had borne children and was young. He saw her again in the softly rolling carriage and in the shop, trying on gloves, and in the café, beside him in the corner, and in the street in the rain. In this one movement, when she raised her arms, lay all her beauty. Her movement simultaneously evoked every aspect of beauty, supplication, disrobing, denial and submission. She lowered her arms. The right hand began to stretch a glove over the left with scrupulous care.

'Stay !' he said suddenly. And he added to this : 'Don't

go!', more gently, tenderly, and a little sharply, as he noticed in self-reproach a moment later.

'All it needs is for me to turn the key, and it's settled.' He saw how Hilde glanced at the door and slowly and scrupulously stripped off her glove again. Now it was an unclothed hand, not just a naked one. It seemed as if he were seeing her for the first time. He took a single rapid step to the door and locked it.

7

Old Herr von Maerker was due to travel on for his cure the next day. Friedrich saw him that evening. The festive glow of the many lamps in the restaurants made his white-haired old age more venerable, his daughter's beauty more radiant. Herr von Maerker looked older than he was, and more important. He resembled old portraits, faces that time has moulded more than nature or art, endowed with the lustre of a melancholy solemnity by the irrevocability of the vanished epochs which they mirror. Herr von Maerker had never been astute. Now, as occasionally happens, his age deputized for wisdom. And, because he was one of those men who have outlived their epoch, he evoked in Friedrich the courteous respect one owes to an old forgotten monument. He did not seem to suspect that Hilde's encounter with Friedrich was other than pure coincidence. But even had he suspected, his respect for his daughter's life and privacy was too great for him to seek to discern relationships that were not voluntarily disclosed to him. Like the men of his generation, he still took it for granted that wives and daughters had a natural instinct for the decorous and the unseemly, for honour and appearance, for reputation and worth. Herr von Maerker still belonged to the last generation of well-mannered Middle Europeans who cannot remain seated when a woman is standing in front of them, who, without venturing a reproof, are continually amazed by the manners of the young, who still speak gracefully while they are eating, and who can still say something sensible without being intelligent themselves, who are chivalrous and harmless and distribute compliments like little declarations of love committing them to nothing. He was aware of his daughter's unhappy marriage, but it did not occur to him to reproach himself for having compelled the Director General to marry Hilde. He had not known his daughter for many a year. Now age made him clear-sighted. But he kept silent, not only because he would have been embarrassed to ask, but because he would have been even more embarrassed to let it be noticed that he possessed the capacity to guess.

'I remember you very well,' he said to Friedrich. 'You visited us once.' Friedrich thought of the candid journalist who had so obstinately assured him that he did not recognize him. 'Much has happened since then. And yet it seems to me that we knew it all beforehand. Year by year I was able to see with my own eyes how the country was disintegrating, how people were becoming indifferent. But malicious too, yes, malicious,' he added. He said this with the hindsight of one beyond the tomb.

'We made jokes, we all laughed at them,' he continued. 'I have to reproach myself for a few. Believe me, jokes alone are enough to destroy an ancient country. All races have mocked. And yet in my time, when the man was more important than his nationality, the possibility existed of making a homeland for all out of the old monarchy. It could have been the prototype in miniature of a great future world, and at the same time the last reminder of a great European era in which North and South had been united. It is all over,' concluded Herr von Maerker, with a slight movement of the hand with which he seemed to disperse the last remnants of his recollections.

Even his sadness was accompanied by serenity. His sombre obituary on his fatherland did not prevent him from enjoying to the full, and with a mild deliberation, his black coffee and thin cigarette and it seemed as if he enjoyed life the more because it still continued beyond his own time, and as if he enjoyed each day, each evening, each meal that heaven granted him with the pleasure one derives from unexpected and unearned holidays. The destruction of the monarchy had put an end only to the active period of his life, he had only ceased to exist as a contemporary, but he continued to live on as the passive observer of a new era which, though it did not please him at all, did not bother him in the slightest because it did not in any way concern him.

He took leave of Friedrich, Hilde accompanied him. They decided to meet again in an hour.

During this hour Friedrich walked up and down in front of the hotel, just as he would have done ten years before. 'Everything's alive again!' he thought. 'Nothing has happened between the day I first saw her in the carriage and today. I am young and happy. Shall I yet believe in the miracle of love? It is obviously a miracle when what has happened is obliterated.'

And then he said to Hilde : 'Once, during my escape from Siberia, I thought of taking you with me to a remote and peaceful country. There are still peaceful foreign countries. Let us be on our way.'

'We do not need them in order to be happy.'

They walked through broad unlighted streets, across animated squares, avoided dangers unthinkingly, only by means of the waxing instinct to remain alive and to live. They would have succeeded in saving themselves from a catastrophe, among a thousand who perished they would have been the only survivors.

He was spared none of the follies with which masculine infatuation is so well endowed. Jealousy possessed him, not so much against particular men but a jealousy for the whole of the long period that Hilde had passed without him. And he even finally asked that most stupid and masculine of all the questions contained in the lexicon of love : 'Why didn't you wait for me?' And he received the inevitable reply, which any other woman would have given, and which is far from a logical answer but rather a continuation of this question : 'I have never loved anyone but you!'

And so love began to lead him from an abnormal to a normal existence, and he got to know its mortal and yet eternal delights and, for the first time in his life, the happiness that consists in giving up great goals in favour of small ones and of overestimating the attainable so extravagantly that there is nothing more to seek. They travelled through white cities, stood in great harbours, saw ships sail for foreign shores, met trains that sped into the unknown, and could never catch sight of a ship or a train without envisaging themselves travelling off into the distance, the future, the void. They anxiously counted the days they could still remain together, and the fewer they became the richer and more full of improbable happenings the remainder seemed to be. If the first week had been an indivisible unit of time, the second already split into days, the third into hours, and in the fourth, in which they began to savour every moment as an entire rich day, they regretted having allowed the first to pass so prodigally.

'I shall follow you everywhere,' said Hilde, 'even to Siberia!'

'Why should I go there? I no longer intend to place myself in dangerous situations.'

'What else do you want to do then?'

'Nothing at all.'

Hilde fell into a deep and disappointed silence. It was the first time that they had suddenly arrived at a point where they ceased to understand each other. These moments recurred more and more often, only they forgot them over again. Both delayed explanations for more favourable opportunities. But such opportunities generally failed to arrive and the silent hours became increasingly common. There were tendernesses that Friedrich did not reciprocate. Words fell from the lips of each without an echo, like stones into a bottomless abyss.

Once she said, perhaps to propitiate him: 'I admire you, for all that.' And he could not restrain himself from replying: 'Whom haven't you admired before now? A painter, a gifted author, the war, the wounded. Now you're admiring a revolutionary.'

'One gets more clever,' she replied.

'One gets more stupid,' he said.

And there began a rapid to-and-fro of empty meaningless words, a battle with empty nutshells.

'She has to have someone to admire,' thought Friedrich. 'At the moment, I am her hero. Too late, too late. She turns to me at a moment when I am beginning to disown myself. I am no longer my old self, I merely continue to play the part – out of chivalry.'

However, it was settled between them that Hilde would leave her husband and children.

'Don't forget,' she said as she got on the train, 'that I shall follow you everywhere. . . .' 'Even to Siberia,' she added as the train began to gather speed.

He could no longer answer.

She was due to join him a week later.

8

Actually, the story of our contemporary, Friedrich Kargan, might have come to a satisfactory ending here, if by that one understands the final homecoming to a loved woman and the prospect of a kind of domestic happiness that offers itself in the last pages of a book. But Friedrich's peculiar destiny, or the inconstancy of his nature with which we have become acquainted in the present account, resisted so gentle an exit from a stormy existence. Some weeks ago we were startled by the news that he and some members of the so-called 'opposition' who, as is generally known, had declared an open resistance to the ruling régime in Russia, had gone to Siberia for a long spell. What occasioned him to suffer once again for a cause of which he was clearly no longer convinced? On the basis of what little we can deduce from the most recent events in his life, we can only surmise and conjecture as follows.

After he had left Hilde, he found a communication from his friend Berzejev. 'I am not sorry,' wrote the latter, 'that I did not follow you abroad, but I regret that I shall presumably never see you again. Call it the sentimentality of a clearly anarchistically disposed man, which no longer embarrasses me now that I have been publicly stripped of the rank of a revolutionary. To console you, let me say that I go into exile compulsorily and yet willingly. If Savelli only suspected how he is actually satisfying my secret yearning, he would probably assign me to a perpetual couriership between Moscow and Berlin as a punishment; I mean to the post of an upholder of culture, a herald of the electrification of the proletariat, its transformation into an efficient middle class. For men like us, Siberia is the only possible abode.'

The same kind of yearning for the edge of the world could equally well have been expressed by Friedrich. Whether one changes the direction of one's life or not does not seem to depend on a voluntary decision. The bliss of having once suffered for a great ideal and for humanity governs our decisions, even after doubt has long made us clearsighted, knowledgeable and without hope. One has gone through the fire and remains marked for the rest of one's life. Perhaps, too, the woman entered Friedrich's life too late. Perhaps his old friend meant more to him than she did.

The old friend – and the same bitterness which nurtured this friendship today, as formerly the same idealism had done. Did they not both walk about with the proud grief of silent prophets, did they not both record in their invisible writing the symptoms of an inhuman and technically accomplished future, whose emblems are the aeroplane and the football and not the hammer and sickle? 'Compulsorily and yet willingly' – as Berzejev wrote – others too made their way to Siberia.

9

That is possibly why Friedrich obeyed the order to come to Moscow. He stood in Savelli's office. It was situated in the often described and, one may say, most feared building in Moscow. A light bare room. The customary portraits of Marx and Lenin were absent from the light-yellow walls. There were three wide comfortable leather chairs, two in front of the large desk and one behind it. Savelli occupied the latter, back to the window, face turned to the door. On the shining plate-glass over the desk there lay nothing but a single blank yellow octavo sheet. The glass reflected the dim sky admitted by the window. It was somewhat surprising, in this cold room which seemed still to be waiting for its furnishings, in which however Savelli had lived for over two years, to tread on a thick soft red carpet that was intended to absorb not only the sound of footsteps but all sound of any kind. Savelli still looked as he did on the morning when he had crossed the frontier. As R. had said of him, he had changed as little as a principle.

'Sit down,' said Savelli to Friedrich.

'Will it take that long?'

'I can't very well sit while you stand.'

'I don't wish to make it comfortable for either of us.' Savelli rose.

'If you wish,' began Savelli, 'you can have company. R. is leaving tomorrow. He is going to Kemi, sixty-five kilometres from Solovetsk. These are, as you know, pleasant islands, 65 degrees north latitude, 36 degrees of longitude east of Greenwich. Their shores are rocky, with romantic ravines. There are eight thousand, five hundred romantics there already. And please, don't despise the monastery, which dates from the fifteenth century. It even has gilded domes. We've only removed the crosses. That should make R. sad.'

'R. is no friend of mine,' replied Friedrich. 'You're mistaken, Savelli. At a very important period, R. was your friend and not mine. You know well enough that I want to be with Berzejev.'

'I'm at a loss where friendships are concerned. R. had his duty to do, like you and me, no more. He does not choose to go on with it – any more than you.'

'There are such things as rewards.'

'Not in our cause. We are not our own historians. I have never received a reward. I am only a tool.'

'You told me that once before.'

'Yes, some twenty years ago. I have a good memory. There was a good friend of yours present then. Would you like to see him?'

Savelli went to the door and said something softly to the guard. The door stayed half-open. A few minutes later Kapturak appeared in its frame. As if he had come for just this purpose, he began :

'Parthagener is dead at last. And I'm alive, as you can see.'

He began to move about the room, as if he had to prove it. Cap on his head, hands behind his back.

'You see, it's not true that Comrade Savelli is ungrateful. Do you remember? I could have got fifty thousand roubles for him once.'

'And what do you earn here?'

'All kind of experiences, experiences. The expenses on the train don't bring in much. Sometimes I accompany people I know well in the sleeping-car. Do you remember how we used to foot it? I couldn't do it any more nowadays. Look!' Kapturak removed his cap and showed his thick snow-white hair, as white as Parthagener's beard used to be.

He accompanied Friedrich to P. Friedrich no longer travelled between decks, nor in a barred railway carriage. Kapturak was sent with him, not out of mistrust but as a guide, and because Savelli possessed a certain relish for underlining the events that depended on his ukase.

10

While these lines are being written, Friedrich is living in P., together with Berzejev. Just as in Kolymsk.

Only P. is a larger town. It must comprise some five hundred inhabitants. And moreover, as a consolation, a man called Baranowicz lives there, a Pole, who has remained in Siberia since his youth of his own free will, without any curiosity about world events, which only reach the walls of his lonely house like a distant echo. He lives as a contented eccentric with his two large dogs, Jegor and Barin, and for several years has given shelter to the beautiful silent Alja, the wife of my friend Franz Tunda, who abandoned her when he left for the West. Foresters and bear-hunters drop in on Baranowicz. Once a year the Jew Gorin comes with new technical devices. On the basis of information received, Friedrich and Berzejev have made friends with Baranowicz. A man one can trust.

And so they lead the old new life as once before. The frost sings in the winter nights. Its melody may remind the prisoners of the secret humming voices of the telegraph wires, the technical harps of civilized countries. The twilights are long, slow and oppressive, and obscure as much as half of the stunted days. What might the friends find to talk about? They no longer have the consolation of being exiled for the cause of the people, to be sure. Let us hope then that they are contemplating escape.

For in our view it is the mark of a disappointed man to suppress his nostalgia for the old solitude and bravely to endure the present in the clamorous void. To determined onlookers like Friedrich, without any hope, the old solitude offers every pleasure : the putrescent smell of water and fish in the winding alleys of old harbour towns, the paradisiacal glitter of lights and mirrors in the cellars where made-up girls and blue sailors dance, the melancholy ecstasy of the accordion, the profane organ of popular desire, the fine and foolish bustle of the wide streets and squares, the rivers and lakes of asphalt, the illuminated

215

green and red signals in the railway stations, those glassed-in halls of yearning. And finally the hard and proud melancholy of a solitary who wanders on the fringes of pleasures, follies and sorrows . . . .

Publisher's Note

The Silent Prophet, first published in Germany in 1966 as *Der Stumme Prophet*, is one of Joseph Roth's most characteristic and revealing works. It is also something of a problem novel in that the manuscript was never revised or prepared for publication in the author's lifetime and did not appear in its present form until twenty-seven years after his death.

Together with *Flucht ohne Ende* (*Flight without End*), 1927, *Zipper und sein Vater*, 1928, and *Rechts und Links*, 1929, it belongs to a group of novels all sharing a theme that was central to the author's own experience and view of life : that of the outsider unable to settle in western European society after the 1914-1918 war. Immediately after these biographical novels with their avowed objectivity and reporting of 'observed fact', and with heroes who all represent some aspect of Roth's own personality (real or imagined), he turned to the freer inventions of works like *Hiob* (*Job*), 1930, and *Radetzkymarsch* (*The Radetzky March*), 1932, for which he is more widely known.

It has been established that Roth was working on the present novel in 1927 and 1928; S. Fischer Verlag, to whom he was briefly under contract, rejected the unfinished manuscript in 1928. This seems to have discouraged Roth, although excerpts from the book appeared in two publications, *24 neue deutsche Erzähler* and *Die Neue Rundschau*, in the following year. We also know that Roth went to Moscow for the *Frankfurter Zeitung* in the autumn of 1926 and became increasingly interested during this trip – as his *Reisebilder* show – in the changes brought about by the Revolution. There is evidence dating from this time of his disappointment with the embourgeoisement of the revolutionary idea and of his own ambivalent feelings towards the superficial allure of western city life, themes which were later to appear in *The Silent Prophet.*

In 1926 there was still much speculation about the fate of Trotsky, but interest died down after the publication of the latter's autobiography in 1929. This may be one of the reasons why Roth decided to lay aside the novel he began after his trip to Russia. It is almost certainly the 'Trotsky novel' he himself referred to in 1938. Although Stalin (Savelli), Lenin, Radek, and Trotsky (T.) appear only as marginal figures in the book there are enough analogies between Friedrich Kargan's fate and that of Trotsky, as it then appeared, to make the link. In his postscript to the German edition, Werner Lengning enlarges on this and also gives an account of how the manuscript came to light and was prepared for publication.

'From the *Reisebilder* we know that Joseph Roth was in Moscow in the winter of 1926 for the *Frankfurter Zeitung.* The scene in the preface to the Kargan novel in the Moscow hotel on New Year's Eve of 1926, indicates the uncertainty about Trotsky's fate which then stirred the world. It was known that, after Lenin's death, Trotsky sharply opposed Stalin, that he lost his post as People's Commissioner for War in January 1925, that he stayed in Berlin in the spring of 1926 – still a member of the Politburo – fell ill there and had to undergo an operation. But one only learned later that, on 16 January, 1927, he was exiled to Alma Ata and, on 20 January, 1929, was expelled from the Soviet Union. . . . Trotsky's autobiography appeared at the end of 1929 and he began his restless wanderings from France by way of Norway to Mexico. From the idol of anti-bourgeois circles in Germany, from the exile who could be sure of general human sympathy and who was possibly preparing his escape, expulsion created an outlaw. The Kargan material, already known through two partial printings of certain passages of Book Three, remained unpublished. Joseph Roth turned to other themes, yet he preserved the manuscript until his death [in Paris in 1939].

'Shortly before aliens were expelled from Paris in the Second World War, his friends Friderike Zweig and Hermann Kesten had given the manuscript they had discovered to Joseph Roth's French translator for safe keeping; then the trail was lost. In the confusion of the war and the post-war period, the Kargan manuscript, together with other effects, came to America, was there salvaged for the second time by Hermann Kesten in 1963, and was handed over to the Leo Baeck Institute in New York with the agreement of the firms of Kiepenheuer & Witsch of Cologne and Allert de Lange of Amsterdam [joint publishers and copyright holders of Roth's work]. With other manuscripts which Hermann Kesten had selected for publication in 1964, the Cologne firm received the photocopies of the Kargan manuscript, the so-called Trotsky novel.

'The initial perusal of photocopies at the firm was discouraging. One had the impression of sheets of manuscript and typescript hurriedly assembled in bundles before the flight, which had resisted all attempts at sorting until then.

'The "Trotsky novel" finally came to the author of this postscript who had already become familiar with Roth's handwriting in the course of deciphering the unpublished letters of Joseph Roth to Stefan Zweig and Blanche Gidon.

'Inspection of what at first appeared as inextricably confused sheets gave a good insight into the working methods of Joseph Roth, who had reworded the novel repeatedly at different times, and finally there emerged two handwritten drafts of the early part of the novel (drafts A and B) and a typescript (draft C), which partly supplement each other. Draft B begins as a copy by Roth of draft A as reworked by him. Typescript C contains further condensed and tightened texts from draft B, but these make up only a third of the novel.

'From the three drafts it became possible to reconstruct the novel continuously as far as Chapter Seven of Book Two. After that point no continuation appears to exist. However, by then the main characters belonging to the Kargan material as well as the line of action had clearly emerged, facilitating the deciphering of script, letter forms, page numbers (mostly scored through but recognizable with the aid of a magnifying glass as being in Roth's hand), and any manuscript sheets not belonging to this novel were eliminated. The result showed that Joseph Roth not only worked on each successive draft of his novels with astonishing thoroughness, but also kept everything – from draft A to draft C – that was superseded at successive creative stages. All the material needed to complete the novel was therefore there. Where Joseph Roth's initial pagination was either missing or illegible, it became necessary, with the aid of a magnifying glass, to test the internal relationship to the still unfinished chapters of Book Two and Book Three and to find the textual link between sheets by means of overlapping sentences. This cumbersome procedure brought the desired result : sheet succeeded sheet in unbroken sequence. Thus it was possible to produce an edition in which there is not a single word that is not by Roth himself.

'It has already been said that version C includes only parts of the novel and goes only as far as the middle of chapter seven of Book Two. From there on only the B version exists, based, up to this point, on the revised portion of the old A version. The present edition therefore relies on the C version for the opening chapters and on the B version for the remaining ones.'